About the Author

Frank Dirscherl (b. 1973) is the Amazon bestselling author of *The Wraith* and editor of *Beyond the Lens*. His series of *The Wraith Adventures* books have been enjoyed by multitudes of readers the world over. Other books in the series include *Valley of Evil*, *Crossfire*, *Cult of the Damned* and *Cry of the Werewolf*, with more to come.

A professionally certified library technician, who has been working in libraries for more than twenty years, Dirscherl has also worked at a medical practice in a data entry position, covered books for a book wholesale company, and as a lecturer to children on the merits, and writing, of comic books.

He lives on the south coast of New South Wales, Australia, with his beautiful wife Jennifer, where he is currently working on his latest piece of fiction.

For more information on Frank, please visit his website at
www.frankdirscherl.com

Praise for *The Wraith*
Amazon bestseller

"I love the coloring job and specially the 'glowing' eyes on the chest of the character."
- Guillermo del Toro, director, *Blade II, Hellboy I & II*

"I liked the story a lot... It's a very strong debut."
Steve Englehart, writer, *Detective Comics, The Avengers, Green Lantern*

"I have read the novel (I couldn't put it down)... It is amazing to see how her (Leena) character evolves from Part I to Part II. At first she appears as every other 'girlfriend' in an action film, but those twelve months that pass obviously change her as a person and I love the person she becomes: tougher, but still human."
- Amber Moelter, actress, *Catwoman: Copycat*

"I finished *The Wraith* book last night. I must say I enjoyed it quite a bit. The scenes kept playing in my head like a big budget Hollywood film. I mentioned earlier that I enjoy when the hero is put to the test physically and doesn't win the battle unscathed. Boy, (Frank) delivered that in spades!"
- Jeff Welborn, artist, *Nightmare World, The Wraith*

"Genius + sweat + dedication = hard hittin' hero action! Go Aussie!"
- Dan Lennard, writer, *People* magazine

"*The Wraith* is a wonderful throwback to the purple prose of the bloody pulps with a hero clearly descendant from the likes of the Shadow and the Spider. A fast, action-packed thrill-ride with great characters, both noble and villainous. Slam-bang kick off to a super new series. One I'm anxious to follow."

> – Ron Fortier, writer, *The Spider, Brother Bones, Domino Lady*

"I became familiar with Frank Dirscherl's The Wraith from the comic book of the same name. When the first Wraith novel came out I just had to read it. I was not disappointed. The Wraith is a fast-paced thrill-ride. I'm looking forward to the upcoming sequel."

> – Bobby Nash, writer, *Evil Ways, Fantastix, Lance Star*

"*The Wraith* (is) a really fun read. Have been a fan of Kenneth Robeson's Doc Savage and The Avenger books for years... *The Wraith* reminds me of Robeson at his best."

> – G.R. Lawson, Publisher, General Jinjur Comics

"A short, pulp, superhero novel... Clearly more adventures to come with how this is set up."

> – Richard Scott, *Super Reader* website

"*The Wraith* is an enlightening journey into the darkness of superhero fiction, and a worthy entry into both pulpdom and comicdom."

> – Kevin Noel Olson, *Silver Bullet Comics* website

"*The Wraith* is a testament to Frank's dedication and talent. Other small press characters have come and gone, but The Wraith endures, because Frank understands what makes a classic character."

- Richard Evans, writer, *The Canadian Legion*

"When it comes to superhero fiction and classic pulp stories, Frank Dirscherl channels those classic adventures of the past into *The Wraith* with ease and gives you a hero to believe in."

- Stephen J. Semones, writer/director, *Beyond the Lens, Crossfire, The Wraith: Eyes of Judgment*

"Frank Dirscherl's writing is action-packed and reminds me why superhero fiction is so much fun in the first place!"

- A.P. Fuchs, writer, *The Axiom-man Saga, The Way of the Fog, Undead World trilogy*

Praise for *Valley of Evil*

"The second Wraith novel is an improvement, I think. Right from the start Dirscherl throws you into the middle of crazy action.... This book is a whole lot of superheroic pulp fun, and the good news is there seems to be more to come...I look forward to some more of the same."

- Richard Scott, *Super Reader* website

"I think (Dirscherl) really captured a noir element with (his) voice."

- Joshua Gamon, writer, *Abigail & Rox, Digital Webbing Presents*

"I did quite enjoy the books. Best of all, it wasn't overly sex-filled or gory—I can't stand most modern superhero comics that show such things or have the heroes just swear and swear. So *The Wraith* (and *Valley of Evil*) was just up my alley."

- Greg Gick, writer, *The Werewolf of Rutherford Grange, Tales of the Shadowmen, Secret Agent X Vol. 2*

"The Dread Avenger is back. After battling the Cobra in his first prose adventure, The Wraith returns to face all new challenges from Metro City's greatest villains, most notably Hong Kong drug kingpin Ma Tzi. As with his first Wraith novel, Frank Dirscherl treats us to a pulp-inspired adventure that keeps readers on the edge of their seat. You have to read this novel in one sitting."

- Bobby Nash, writer, *Evil Ways, Fantastix, Lance Star*

"In the past five years there has been a tremendous resurgence in pulp fiction centering on the old heroic pulps. Young writers have started taking up the mantle of old masters like Walter Gibson and Lester Dent and begun creating their own avengers in tales of genuine purple prose. Among the best of this new generation of wordsmiths is Australian, Frank Dirscherl and the exploits of his modern pulp paladin, The Wraith. This is grand pulp!"

   – Ron Fortier, writer, *The Spider, Brother Bones, Domino Lady*

Praise for *Crossfire*

"Stephen did a fantastic job of bringing Frank Dirscherl's character to life!"
- Adam DiTroia, composer, *The Wraith: Eyes of Judgment*,
MTV, Fox Sports

"Loved the book!! Can't wait for the next installment..."
- Larry Mainland, actor, *The Walking Dead, Lawless,
The Three Stooges*

"The action comes swift, and doesn't stop until the final pages. *Crossfire* tells a great story of betrayal and revenge."
- C.R. Blevins, writer, *A Western Tale*

Praise for *Cult of the Damned*

"Only by the first three pages, Frank Dirscherl wonderfully captures a dark and mysterious atmosphere, one that leaves the reader with a cryptic and eerie sensation; one that makes me cold just thinking about it."

- Rennie Cowan, writer/director, *The Thriller Idol: A Tribute to the Legacy of Michael Jackson, Kade the Conqueror*

"Frank Dirscherl pulls you into the world of The Wraith from the first sentence and refuses to let you go until the last one."

- Stephen J. Semones, writer/director, *Beyond the Lens, Crossfire, The Wraith: Eyes of Judgment*

"The Wraith is one of my favorite characters and every time Frank Dirscherl puts pen to paper I know I'm in for a real treat."

- A.P. Fuchs, writer, *The Axiom-man Saga, The Way of the Fog, Undead World trilogy*

Praise for *Cry of the Werewolf*

"Frank Dirscherl delivers beyond measure... The solid characters, settings and story really propel you page to page and leave you hanging on for more."
- Stephen J. Semones, writer/director, *Beyond the Lens, Crossfire, The Wraith: Eyes of Judgment*

"Each new installment in *The Wraith Adventures* series is a guaranteed good time filled with high adventure, romance and pulpy fun. Dirscherl is at the top of his form."
- A.P. Fuchs, writer, *The Axiom-man Saga, The Way of the Fog, Undead World trilogy*

Praise for *Werewolves Attack!* in *Metahumans vs Werewolves*

"Always a great read. Can never put it down once you get started... "

– Geraldine L. Lewis, writer, Amazon

Praise for *Zombies Attack!* in *Metahumans vs the Undead*

"This compilation of superheroes vs evil offers top entertainment for superhero lovers! Frank Dirscherl and others are at their best with their contributed stories. I will now pursue other stories written by these authors, such as those involving Mr. Dirscherl's The Wraith. This type of reading enjoyment knows no end!"

- Ramona Wingart, writer, *Where is Brother Beaver?, Emily Suzanne Smith!*

By Frank Dirscherl

Fiction

Titles in *The Wraith Adventures* series
(in story order)
The Wraith
Valley Of Evil
Crossfire (edited)
Cult of the Damned
Cry of the Werewolf
Werewolves Attack! in *Metahumans vs Werewolves* (short story)
Zombies Attack! in *Metahumans vs the Undead* (short story)

Attack of the Birdman in *Lance Star – Sky Ranger Vol. 1* (short story)

Non-Fiction

*The Wraith: Eyes of Judgment – The Official Script Book
& Movie Guide* (with Stephen Semones)
Waterfall After Dark in *The Hitchers of Oz* (short story)
Beyond the Lens (edited)

Comic Books

The Wraith #0
The Wraith: The Collected Editions #1-3
Curse of the Cortes Stone (with Joe Martino & Scott Story)

www.trinitycomics.com

CULT OF THE DAMNED

The Wraith Adventures #3

by

Frank Dirscherl

TRINITY COMICS
WOLLONGONG

TRINITY COMICS
PO Box 31
Wollongong NSW 2520

ISBN 978-0-646-90824-3

PUBLISHED BY TRINITY COMICS, August 2013
www.trinitycomics.com
FRONT COVER PENCILS by Jeff Welborn
FRONT COVER INKS by Jeff Austin
FRONT COVER COLORS by Splash!
COVER LAYOUT AND DESIGN AND INTERIOR DESIGN by Frank Dirscherl
FIRST PUBLISHED IN 2009
SECOND EDITION

For more on *Cult of the Damned*
visit www.trinitycomics.com

Text set in Garamond. Printed and bound in the USA

National Library of Australia Cataloguing-in-Publication entry

Author: Dirscherl, Frank, 1973- author.

Title: Cult of the damned / by Frank Dirscherl

Edition: Second edition

ISBN: 9780646908243 (paperback)

Series: Wraith adventures ; 3.

Subjects: The Wraith (Fictitious character)
Superheroes.

Dewey Number: A823.4

For Jennifer with all my love forever

CULT OF THE DAMNED

~ Prologue ~

The rain pummeled down from the night sky in sheets as thick as lead. The furious onslaught from the heavens lashed the windshield of the armored truck as it rumbled down the busy Metro City thoroughfare. Life never took a breather in a city like Metro, and even at 4 A.M. in such inclement weather, the streets were teeming with people and cars of all descriptions. Car horns blared, certain people—johns, hookers, bums, cops—mill about, yelling, weeping, running, fighting. Night was always a bleak time in Metro City, and this night was no exception.

"Man, what a time to be delivering this cargo," Ralph said from the passenger seat of the armored truck. "Why the heck do we get stuck with all the crap jobs, Jim?" Ralph was a burly, heavy-set man in his fifties with a full, graying mustache and heavily-lidded eyes. He shifted uncomfortably in his seat, while his partner peered intently through the windshield, trying to keep control of the truck in the appalling conditions.

Jim shrugged his shoulders. "And why do we have to deliver this thing at this ungodly hour?"

"Because Mr. Latham told us to," said Ralph, who noted Jim's sour expression. He sighed. "Mr. Latham thought it best to deliver such valuable cargo at a time when there was the least chance of anything going wrong. That work better for you?"

Jim, younger, slimmer and less hairy than his co-pilot, arched an eyebrow. "Yeah, but that doesn't reflect well on us though, does it? I can't wait to get rid of it. Darn thing gives me the creeps."

"Ah well. Latham pays for the service, so who are we to argue?"

"What is it exactly anyway?" Jim queried. "Some voodoo piece?"

"I don't know, and I don't really care. All I know is we were warned it shouldn't be touched under any circumstances. Something about it being dangerous. Beats me how, though."

Jim shivered at the mention of the word *dangerous*.

The truck inched its way through the torrential rain, down the hectic Montgomery Street, swarming as it was with that particular brand of nightlife for which Metro had long since become infamous. Red light turning green, Jim veered into the narrower Harris Street, and then out into the wider expanse of Joseph Boulevard.

"Are you sure we're going the right way?" Jim asked, guiding the truck as best he could down the wide, lengthy road. He fiddled with the de-frost controls on the truck's dashboard, trying to get it working but without much luck. The windshield was fogged over.

"Yeah, yeah, turn here," Ralph replied. He removed a handkerchief from his right-side trouser pocket, and wiped the windshield clear as best he could.

Jim moved the truck onto George Avenue and finally toward the looming Metro City Gallery. The lights of the gallery shone through the foggy windshield in bright blotches as the truck turned and drove carefully up the short drive, coming to a halt at a security gate.

Jim wound down his window. "Hey, where do we deliver this?" he asked the guard in the small booth beside them.

"You the special delivery guys?" the guard shouted above the din of the pouring rain. Jim nodded. "Go round the turn there and then head to the back." The guard thumbed to somewhere further down the drive.

"Yeah, okay. Sure thing," Jim said and rolled up the window. "I'll be glad to hand this stuff over and get back home. I can just catch a few hours sleep before my next shift. I hate night shifts." He drove the truck further down the drive as directed.

"Especially in this kind of weather," Ralph said. "You think it's ever going to stop raining? How long's it been, two weeks? I'm practically growing gills already."

"I read in the paper it's expected to rain most of this month. Climate change they call it," Jim said, as he parked the truck in the circular loading zone protected from the elements by a large overhead awning. "C'mon, let's get this over with."

The two security officers exited the truck and moved back to the vehicle's rear door, the sound of their footsteps barely distinguishable from that of the rain. They looked up to see a tall, well-dressed man with thinning hair and a grin that would make the Cheshire Cat green with envy approaching them from the gallery's loading dock. He was flanked by several uniformed armed guards, ready to take possession of the truck's goods.

"Gentlemen, my name is Bartholomew Gregory. I'm the curator of this gallery," greeted the curator in a hearty tone. "I am so glad to see you've arrived with our invaluable artifact."

"What is this we're hauling, exactly? Some voodoo stone or something?" Jim asked while opening the truck's rear door.

"An artifact that is absolutely priceless," Gregory said, still smiling. "The Cortes Stone, an ancient Aztec stone carving, depicting one of their gods, Huitzilopochtli, defeating the invading Spaniards led by Hernando Cortes. It was only recently discovered in the wilds of Mexico in a heretofore undiscovered tomb. Our great patron, Robert Latham ensured this international treasure would make its home here as part of this city's two-hundredth anniversary celebration."

Ralph looked to Jim and rolled his eyes. Jim knew what he meant. *Is this guy reading off a cue card?*

"Well, here's your precious carving, packed away nice and tight," Ralph said, indicating inside the truck.

"I cannot thank you enough for your vigilance and speedy arrival here. I shall make sure Mr. Latham hears of your exemplary work," Gregory said. The curator indicated his own guards to take charge of the situation, which they promptly did, surrounding the truck carefully, their guns raised in readiness for any eventuality. From the rear of the loading dock several workmen appeared, dressed in overalls, one of whom pulled a metallic trolley behind him.

"Uh, yeah, well, thanks," Ralph said, scratching his head with the one hand while brandishing a clipboard with the other. "Now, if you could just sign here, Mr.—"

"Over there, please be careful with the package," Gregory shouted to one of the workmen, ignoring Ralph. "It's your jobs if you drop it."

Two of the workmen climbed into the truck and removed the fastenings securing the wooden crate to the truck floor. They then carefully shifted the large crate to the edge of the truck, then onto the awaiting trolley.

"Now, let's get this inside and away from this atrocious weather," Gregory said, turning on his heels and quickly making his way back into the gallery. The workmen, with the secured carving, followed suit, the gallery's security guards remaining on alert.

"Uh...Mr. Gregory?" Ralph shouted, waving his clipboard. "Could you—" But Gregory had already disappeared, vanishing within the bowels of the city gallery. Ralph looked to Jim, who merely shrugged his shoulders. "C'mon, we have to get this guy's signature before we can leave."

They strode the path down into the loading dock and climbed the stairs up into the main loading area. They were greeted by a plethora of crates and boxes of all sizes and lighting so low as to be almost sinister, the boxes and crates casting eerie shadows on the walls surrounding them.

"Where'd they get to?" Jim asked, stumbling around in the darkness.

"Over there." Ralph pointed. "There's some light."

The two arrived at a partially-open wooden door. A weak light shone from the other side. Peering round, Jim saw a long, narrow corridor snaking down toward a murky center.

"Take a look," Jim said and let Ralph grab a peek.

"I guess they went that way," Ralph said, again scratching his head.

They passed through the corridor, entered the larger, darkened room beyond, then heard voices coming from yet another room, the entrance to which lay ahead of them.

"This way. Let's just get this signed so we can get outta this maze," Ralph muttered.

They passed through this last doorway to find themselves in a large, cavernous area with high glass ceilings and low, moody lighting. The rain beat down on the glass, its steady drum rumbling throughout the room. Paintings and etchings of incredible beauty and intricacy lined the walls. Bartholomew Gregory and three of his workmen stood at the far side of the room. The armed guards were nowhere in sight.

"Careful. The stone is the most precious piece we've ever received," Gregory said.

As the two security officers walked over to join him, two of the three workmen cautiously pried open the wooden crate containing the carving.

"Mr. Gregory, we need your—" Ralph started to say but was cut off by a wave of the hand.

"Hmm...? Oh, yes, one moment please," the curator replied absently.

With the wooden crate open, a gloved workman lifted a small, rounded, stone slab roughly twelve inches in diameter above the rim of the crate. Gregory's eyes shone bright at the sight of it. The surface of the stone was decorated with carvings of unique and complex beauty, with depictions of various figures that neither Jim nor Ralph recognized.

"It's even more beautiful than I could have ever imagined," Gregory said under his breath. "See the great sun god wreaking vengeance on the Conquistadors? And here," he indicated to one of the figures on the carving, "on Cortes himself. A depiction of the Aztec Indians greatest desire, and one which they sadly never realized." He stopped to catch his breath. "And the jade embossing the rim...it is an amazing piece." Gregory straightened. "Put it over there." And nodded toward the stand, shaped much like a speaker's lectern, nearby.

The workman holding the stone laid it gently into its ready-made cradle at the top of the stand.

"Good," Gregory said, still marveling over the stone. "I find I cannot take my eyes off this. It's as though I..."

He moved closer to the object. "I need to—" He reached out to touch the carving, to run his fingers along its elaborate imagery of godly vengeance.

"Mr. Gregory, no!" Ralph cried.

But it was too late.

Gregory's face lit up in apparent ecstasy as he felt the texture of the stone and its carvings, then lurched backward, coughing, his body heaving violently. He collapsed in a heap on the gallery floor—and quickly disintegrated into ash before the shocked eyes of those present.

~ Chapter 1 ~

Paul Sanderson stood leaning up against the frame of the large bay window within his study library, staring out onto the expansive grounds of his estate. He watched the continuing torrent of rain, which was now getting into its third week. The grounds were lush with growth; despite the rain, the weather was still quite warm and the vegetation was responding in kind. It was morning, though one could hardly tell, the chunky buildup of clouds all but obliterating the sun from view.

At the sound of someone approaching, Paul turned slightly.

"Darling, come to breakfast," Leena Patterson said as she entered the handsomely furnished room.

Leena. The love of his life and partner in his crusade to fight evil wherever they encountered it.

"Hmm. In a moment, darling," Paul replied.

Leena came up beside him. He faced her, noticing a familiar look of concern etched on her attractive features. He gazed into her blue eyes, her oval-shaped glasses, he thought, only enhancing their sparkle. Her shoulder length strawberry blond hair was incredibly beautiful. Her full lips bespoke of a beauty and passion that continued to take his breath away even now, several years since he met her. He couldn't help but smile.

"Paul, what's wrong?" she asked.

"I don't know. Maybe it's the weather. We've barely seen the sun in over two weeks. I know I often dwell in the darkness, but..."

Leena wrapped her arms around him, gave him a quick kiss. "The weather's been unusually dreary of late, but–that's not it. I know you too well."

Paul smiled again. She *did* know him well. He'd loved her for years, long before he'd taken up the mantle of The Wraith and his alter ego, multi-millionaire Paul Sanderson. Back then he was simply Michael Reeve, beat cop, valiantly fighting the good fight within a morass of evil and corruption, both in and out of the police force. But ever since his life had taken that strange twist–fate some would call it–ever since the original Wraith had endowed him with the power and memories the first Dread Avenger possessed, he and Leena had somehow become closer, more attuned to each other. More in love. In many ways, he couldn't make sense of why that was. But in other ways it made perfect sense. In any case, she was right. There *was* something wrong, though it was not something he could place at present.

"It's just a feeling I have, deep in my gut," he said finally.

"What kind of feeling?"

"Something's in the air. I can feel it, almost smell it. Something dangerous." He turned and concentrated his focus once again out onto the estate. "Evil."

* * * * * *

In Robert Latham's study at home, the ornate grandfather clock chimed 6 A.M. as he angrily paced amongst the busts of the great dictators he so admired, with his deputy, Charlie Grieco, watching on. Both were outfitted in superb, and obviously expensive, Brioni double-breasted suits. While Grieco was a younger, slimmer and somewhat slicker version of Latham himself, they could indeed have passed for father and son, such was the similarity in their dress and demeanor.

Latham's study was opulently and eccentrically furnished, the walls covered with plush Persian rugs and tapestries, chairs lined with luxurious Spanish leather, tables and shelves made from deep mahogany and a plethora of bric-a-brac items from all over the world amongst them—a mish-mash of styles and colors that he reveled in. All of the finest quality money could buy.

"Dammit, Charlie, how could this have happened? I was told Gregory was made aware of the danger the stone posed," Latham said sharply.

"He was," Grieco said. "The two security officers who witnessed the...*event*...described the situation as though Mr. Gregory was possessed, acting without thought, as if he'd lost his free will."

"That's nonsense! There's been no reports of the stone having any such power, apart from the obvious. We've been well apprised that the stone cannot be handled without wearing protective clothing. Legend tells us the Cortes Stone will kill those unbelievers who dare touch it. That was borne out of its discovery, with over half the archaeological team dying horribly, and now last night again. Gregory let his zeal override his common sense." Latham pinched the bridge of his nose. "This could become a major public relations nightmare, Charlie. We're not going to let that happen, now, are we?"

"No, Mr. Latham," he said, somewhat subdued. "I'll handle it."

"Good, you do that." Latham took a seat at his oversized, paper-littered desk. He took a cigar—an expensive Cuban—from the small container at the upper right-hand corner, removed the band, snipped the tip, and lit it, blowing the smoke upwards with great satisfaction. "And can we ensure this won't happen again?"

"It'll be done," Grieco said, and exited the study promptly.

"The fools," Latham said to himself under his breath. He unfurled the broadsheet newspaper lying on his desk and peered at the headline:

LATHAM SAVES CITY CELEBRATION! RARE ARTIFACT TO ARRIVE TODAY!

He smiled, as he started to blow rings of smoke from his stogie.

* * * * * *

Detectives Bob Sloan and his partner Rosa Perez both entered the workroom of the Metro City Police Headquarters, exhausted. The burly, broad-shouldered Sloan removed his rain-sodden overcoat and sagged into the chair behind his desk, his pug-nosed features contorted in a mixture of frustration and fatigue.

"No clues; nothing," he said wearily. "There's a serial killer loose in this city, and he's left no clues behind at all."

Perez, her own wet overcoat removed and placed on a nearby stand, propped herself on the end of his desk. She was a tough, Latina woman in her late-twenties. "We do know one thing though: the murders weren't committed where the bodies were found. Howard Boynce has said they were murdered hours earlier and their bodies were dumped later."

"But clues, Perez, we need clues," Sloan said, frustration in his voice. "Some nut is killing innocent people and cutting their hearts out. And we have nothing to go on."

"They're obviously intelligent, though, Bob. Think about it. No clues? Whoever's responsible may be a nut, but they're not stupid."

Sloan nodded in weary agreement. Perez knew her partner all too well—he was the most passionate cop she knew, and as professional and experienced as he was, he always took their cases personally. *Always.* It often made him a tough man to be around, but to her mind, that was also what made him a great cop.

Sloan rubbed his face and eyes, no doubt trying to somehow rid the exhaustion from his body. "Okay...what *do* we have? Summary: ten bodies, all male, have been discovered at various locations throughout the city—"

"The victims appear to have no connection whatsoever with each other, nor do the locations of the bodies shed any light on this nor give any reason as to why they were targeted," Perez added.

"Each victim," Sloan started again, "had their throat cut from ear to ear, and their heart removed—"

"Violently. Clearly the person responsible has no skill with a knife."

"The weapon appears to be either a very long knife or sword of some kind. Howard and the lab boys can't narrow it down any further than that. The murders took place several hours before the bodies were discovered. The serial killer theory is the most valid so far, though we can't discount the cult angle, particularly in light of the potential intelligence level at work here. They may be using the hearts in their ceremonies," Sloan continued.

"We're currently looking into the latter theory as well. Metro has its fair share of wackos," Perez said.

"You're telling me. This bloody rain is even starting to drive *me* insane." He sighed, pausing briefly before continuing. "Today's victim was a Mr. Juan Alehc, forty three year-old plumber from Gladstone. Bachelor, no family of his own apart from his mother, who is living in a nursing home. Juan liked to keep fit and was popular amongst his friends and with the ladies. He had no known enemies. And, as with the other nine victims, there doesn't appear to be anything to connect him with any of them."

"Random attacks," she said. "Though only men are being targeted. That has to mean something."

"You mean our killer is a woman?"

"Not necessarily. But why not? It's not unprecedented."

"No, you're right. And yet..."

"And yet what?"

Sloan shifted in his seat. "I know the serial killer angle is our best bet, and one I'm not yet willing to give up on. But...there's something *more* to this, something sinister. Something I can't quite put my finger on." He stood and Perez saw the intensity in his eyes, knowing full well the level of determination he was now feeling to get to the bottom of this. "But I will, Perez. I will."

~ Chapter 2 ~

The humming of the intricate computerized machinery before him was as incessant as it was strangely hypnotic. When he was at work—which was often—he could sit there for hours, analyzing, investigating and communicating, with barely a thought for the passing of time.

Paul sat at the command center in the heart of the Lair, which was located within and underneath the sizable Sanderson House. He sat there with great consternation. His contacts within the city had alerted him to the terrible news: a tenth victim was found today, mutilated as all the others, with the heart removed and no longer with the body. His stomach churned at the thought of a madman running loose in his city. He'd faced such incredible evil before, but the loss of innocent life never lessened its impact on him; indeed, it spurred him ever forward.

"Darling?" Leena's voice came from behind him.

Lost in a myriad of thoughts, he hadn't noticed her entering the Lair via the secret bookcase entry from the library above.

"It's time to get dressed."

Paul swiveled in his seat. "Dressed?"

"The gala unveiling of the Cortes Stone at the City Gallery tonight. It's the first major event of the two-hundredth anniversary celebration this year, and Robert Latham has promised a grand show," she said.

Paul grimaced at the mention of his great nemesis. "You know his spiel off by heart," he said.

To the outside world, Latham appeared a respectable businessman, the head of a large conglomerate—Latham Industries—involved in everything from electronics to multimedia interests to fossil fuels. He was also well known for his charitable endeavors, ranging from cancer research to the beautification of Metro City. What the majority of the city's population did not know, however, was that Latham was also the head of the largest, most powerful crime cartel on the Eastern seaboard. He was the monstrous spider at the center of the city's insidious web of crime, and everything that was evil and corrupt reverberated in some measure back to him.

"I know how you feel about Latham," Leena said, seeming to catch his change in expression. "But I also know how valuable these forays can be for us. Perhaps we can engage in a little surreptitious detective work tonight?"

Paul smiled. He liked the way she thought. "Lead the way, McDuff."

* * * * * *

The City Gallery was bathed in powerful, mobile spotlights of red, green and blue. Banners promoting the new exhibition were unfurled along the building's eastern side, and the large, circular drive was filled with limousines, Rolls Royces, Bentleys, Mercedeses and other finest of the finest automobiles.

Max Horton slowly pointed the Sanderson Daimler up the drive, navigating the quagmire of parked and moving vehicles, up to the gallery's oval-shaped front entrance. Men and women, superbly outfitted, exited their cars and made their way into the gallery.

"'Tis a fancy affair," Max said. Tonight, Max played chauffeur, as he always did at events such as this, but the stocky Irishman was so much more. Not only was he Paul's chief assistant in his war on crime, and the one responsible for the myriad equipment The Wraith used in that war, but he was also the Sanderson head mechanic, keeping the many vehicles Paul owned in tip-top shape.

"You be careful in there," Max said, cocking his head toward the back seat.

"Park the car. I'll let you know if we need you," Paul said.

"Gotcha, Chief," Max replied, stopping the car at the gallery front entrance.

A resplendently uniformed doorman opened the Daimler's rear door, allowing Paul and Leena to exit like movie stars attending a star-studded Hollywood premiere. Paul was outfitted in a stylish Shanghai C&G tailored dinner jacket, while Leena wore a sparkling, highly-slit black Prada dress, perfectly highlighting the shape and suppleness of her toned body. Paul handed the doorman their embossed invitation.

"This way through the front entrance, Mr. Sanderson. The guests are only now arriving," the doorman said.

Paul held out his arm to Leena. She took it and they made their way up the short flight of steps leading to the revolving glass door at the top.

"You look very handsome," she said, smiling. "I always love how you look in a tux."

"Thank Amy," Paul said, referring to his Shanghai-based tailor, head of Shanghai C&G Fashion Limited, and good friend. He smiled back at her. Paul, who had been in need of a new tailor for some time, actually came across Amy Yang's bespoke business online. They later met when he had been to China on business, liked what he saw and they struck up an arrangement from there.

Upon entering the lavishly decorated gallery, Paul carefully scanned his surroundings. The gallery had recently undergone major renovations, funded by Latham himself as his way of advancing the arts in Metro City. Just what Latham truly knew of the arts, Paul could only wonder. He looked briefly at the ravishing beauty alongside him and smiled once again. Leena caught his glance and returned his smile with one of her own.

"Thank goodness the rain has relented for the time being," she said.

Moving further inside, the two were met by a group of Metro City's finest: the mayor, Police Commissioner George Harrison (wearing his toupee for the occasion), other local politicians, and the rich and famous that made the city their home.

Paul and Leena did the rounds, greeting the people they knew, making small talk with captains of industry, wealthy philanthropists and city officials alike. Waiters that wouldn't look out of place at Buckingham Palace strolled throughout, their trays filled with canapés adorned with Beluga caviar and smoked salmon, while others carried trays of exquisite crystal flutes and piccolos, all containing the finest of French champagnes.

Paul and Leena graciously accepted a proffered flute each.

"Latham sure does know how to put on a good show," Leena said to Paul under her breath, smiling as she took a sip from her glass. "This must have cost him a small fortune."

"But what is he really up to?" Paul whispered back, glancing quickly at his Christopher Ward C60 Trident automatic watch. "He would never go to this expense out of the kindness of his heart. He's profiting from this somehow."

"Perhaps we can find that out tonight."

With no sign of Latham in sight, Paul and Leena continued meandering amongst the crowd, occasionally keeping an eye out for the businessman-cum-crime lord. The walls of the large, central, circular promenade were lined with treasures of incalculable value—paintings by Gainsborough, Constable, Turner, Degas, Monét, Rubens and Rembrandt, and frescoes even Paul did not recognize.

While he took a closer look at a particularly garish painting by Lucien Freud, Commissioner Harrison approached them.

"Paul, Leena, it's wonderful to see you tonight," Harrison said, clearly genuinely delighted to see them. "It's been such a while." He took Paul's hand and shook it with a strong grip. "I'd almost thought you'd gone back to your reclusive ways."

"No chance of that, Commissioner," Paul replied with a smile. "Especially not on a night such as this."

"Yes, Robert Latham does know how to impress," Harrison said, fiddling with his collar. "Speaking of Latham, has anyone seen him? The show appears to be running without him."

"Oh, I don't think that's really possible," Leena said.

"Commissioner, I'd like to speak to you about these murders—" Paul began.

"Ladies and gentlemen," the voice of Robert Latham boomed out over a microphone. The assemblage of people turned in the direction of the voice. Latham stood in the center of a spotlight shining down at the rear of the promenade. He smiled broadly once he'd gained everyone's attention. "Thank you all for coming tonight. Proceeds of this fine gala go, of course, to my cancer foundation, so thank you once again for your patronage." The crowd clapped, and Latham waited a brief moment for the applause to die down. "I know why you're all here though, and I can well understand it. The Cortes Stone has been a phenomenal find, one that has both thrilled and amazed the artistic and scientific communities. And I am equally thrilled to be able to announce tonight its *permanent* home here in Metro City."

The crowd cheered, this time a little more exuberantly.

"Where's Bartholomew Gregory?" Paul whispered in Leena's ear. "Knowing him, he would have been reveling in this."

She nodded in acknowledgment but said nothing in reply.

"I don't want to keep you waiting any longer," Latham continued. "I know how anxious you must all be. So, without further ado, here it is—the Cortes Stone!"

Latham stepped to one side, the spotlight moving only slightly backward, resting upon a slender pedestal encased in a circular Perspex dome at the top. The Cortes Stone was inside. An audible hum emanated from the crowd as the large group caught sight of the fabled stone carving. Two armed guards then appeared as if from nowhere and stood alert, transfixed on either side of the pedestal.

"Don't be shy," Latham announced. "The Cortes Stone will remain here on display for all to see until the two hundredth anniversary gala street parade in a few weeks time."

The crowd cheered again, applauding with such force that some in the crowd were forced to reach up and shield their ears. Paul scowled at Latham, who stood beside the Cortes Stone, basking in the praise of Metro City's finest.

"It bothers you, doesn't it?" Leena said, having noted his expression.

"You know it does," Paul replied under his breath. "These people don't know who Latham really is. They believe the façade."

They made their way carefully through the shifting throng toward the Cortes Stone. It took a little while—for everyone wanted at least a glimpse of the fabled stone—but upon eventually reaching it, Paul bent over to get a closer look. The brilliant jade around the rim of the stone caught his eye immediately; it dazzled as though powered by a luminescence of its own. The carvings themselves were as intricate and detailed as they were fascinating. Paul, through the extensive worldwide travel of his predecessor, was conversant with many cultures, both current and obscure, and was familiar with the Aztec civilization. The scene of the Cortes-led Spaniards being struck down by the vengeful god Huitzilopochtli amazed him.

A radical case of wish fulfillment if ever there was one, he thought.

"Remarkable, isn't it?" Latham said, bending over to match Paul's gaze on the stone.

"Indeed it is, Robert," he replied, straightening. "You're to be congratulated for acquiring this treasure and bringing it to Metro."

"Nothing a little bribing and exhorting couldn't accomplish," Latham chuckled. "Those Mexicans were a bit of a nuisance, I must admit."

Paul and Leena smiled.

"Nothing is impossible for you, Robert," Paul said with a minor bite to his words.

"Too right, Sanderson. Too right. I'm glad you see right through me."

"I'm surprised Bartholomew Gregory isn't here." Paul reached for another glass of champagne from the tray of a passing waiter. "We all know how active he was in promoting this fine event. I hope he's not ill."

Latham's face clouded over, though Paul wasn't certain if the reaction was genuine or not.

"Unfortunately, Bartholomew tendered his resignation only yesterday. He has a heart condition and decided it best to retire immediately in the interests of his health and family. He's disappointed he couldn't be here tonight, of course, but we all understand that his health and family come first." Latham seemed sincere. "And I was only too willing to step into the breach to take his place as master of ceremonies."

"Of course, Robert," Leena said. "We understand. I just hope Bartholomew is all right. Could you please extend our best wishes?"

"Be glad to," Latham replied quickly, his demeanor shifting back to the celebratory in an instant. "Now, if you'll excuse me, other guests are waiting."

He sauntered past Paul and Leena and merged with a large section of the crowd at the center of the gallery's main promenade, smiling and accepting congratulations with equal measure.

Paul touched Leena's arm. "Something's not right. Gregory retiring due to heart problems?"

"It's not impossible," she said.

"No, but just the same, something's not right here. I can feel it. Something's happened to Gregory and Latham's covering it up. But what could it be?"

Before she had a chance to respond, an explosion blasted away the gallery's front entrance, sending a multitude of people hurtling through the air. Everyone started to panic, screaming and bunching together, trying to find the nearest exit all at once. Paul and Leena, a little back from the crowd, stood stiffly, their muscles tensed, waiting.

A great billow of smoke erupted from the debris of the front door, filling the gallery. Paul noted it seemed to be moving as if it had a life of its own; this wasn't a mere fire.

"Paul, what's happening?" Leena asked, stunned.

He eyed the expanding plume of smoke carefully. The hair on his neck began to stand on end. A few moments more, and a bulky shape appeared within the smoke. As it moved— floated—toward the people, its form became more and more discernible. A hulking figure at least seven feet tall and clad in filthy, tattered tan robes, emerged from the cloud, its face completely obscured by a ragged, low-hung hood.

Paul immediately noticed the creature's hands.

They were skeletal!

~ Chapter 3 ~

The creature stood there silently amidst the mass of people lying on the ground and those standing. It turned its head slowly from side to side as if searching for something before finally settling its gaze on the Cortes Stone to Paul's left.

"Defilers of the sacred stone," the creature said with a voice so deep, so hollow, that it caused even Paul to shudder briefly. "You are disbelievers, not fit to be in the presence of such as this." It pointed toward the stone with a bony finger, the smoke swirling around the creature as though it was being controlled by it. "The stone must be returned from whence it came, and its desecraters punished!"

A security guard to the creature's right suddenly decided to take action, pulling his gun from its holster and waving it at the monster.

"Stop right there, Mister!" the officer said, though Paul detected a hint of shakiness in his voice despite his courage. "I don't know who you are, but—"

The security guard had moved too close. The creature reached out with a skeletal hand, grabbed the hapless guard by the arm, touching his skin. The guard screamed. His face contorted in agony and horror...then he fell away, decaying into a putrid pile of bubbling flesh on the gallery floor.

The sounds of terror and panic filled Paul's ears.

"Disbelievers will be dealt with until the stone is returned and the Aztec Empire restored," the creature boomed.

Aztec Empire? Paul thought. *The empire was conquered by the Spaniards five hundred years ago. How could this nut restore it? It's not possible.*

The creature floated toward the Cortes Stone and Paul, the supernatural smoke sticking to it like glue. Paul remained steadfast, clenching his fists in readiness. He broke from Leena's side, stepping defiantly in front of the Cortes Stone.

"Infidel," the creature said. "Step aside or your fate will match Robert Latham's."

Paul's eyes narrowed, his jaw clenched. "No," he said firmly.

The creature tightened its bony fists, moved closer to Paul, its intent all too obvious. At this range, he could make out a pair of blood-red eyes shimmering within the blackness of the creature's hood.

How do I stop this thing? The creature moved slowly yet surely. *Is it even human?*

A cacophony of sirens broke the silence and cracked the tension in the air. A few seconds more and voices came from outside. Paul recognized the loudest of these as his former police colleague and friend Bob Sloan.

"You in there! We have you surrounded. There's no way out. Exit slowly from the front entrance. Now!"

Sloan shouted through the loudspeaker.

The creature stared at Paul, its skeletal hands still curled into fists, then quickly floated over to the glass-enclosed balcony to its right. It raised its right hand and the entire wall of glass shattered as though it had been hit by a ballistic missile.

The creature turned briefly to face the crowd, its blood-red eyes glowing hot with rage. "The warning has been given, there will not be another. Now there will be only vengeance. So swears" —the creature began to recede through the opening it had created, moving with the ease of a leaf floating down to the ground— "Aztekoth!" And the creature was gone, its ethereal smoke beginning to dissipate.

Sloan's voice again rang out a warning, but it was too late.

Aztekoth had escaped.

Paul jumped out onto the balcony, trying to catch any sign of Aztekoth, but there was none.

It just simply vanished. A shudder ran up Paul's spine.

"Is everyone all right?" Latham called out, emerging from behind the safety of a marble pillar. He strode purposefully through the still-shocked crowd, helping some stunned members up off the floor, seeming to notice some that appeared seriously wounded. He yanked a prone security guard to his feet. "Andy, get the paramedics here, and get out there and alert the police that...that thing escaped."

The guard, shaken, complied, racing through the destroyed front entrance out to the assembled police force.

Leena joined Paul on the balcony, treading carefully amongst the many shards of glass coating the floor.

"What just happened here?" Leena asked, her eyes still wide apparent shock. "I can't believe—I..."

Paul took her in his arms. While she had been well trained to work beside him in innumerable situations, her distress and exasperation, he thought, were only natural under the circumstances.

"I can't explain what we just saw, but trust me, we're going to get to the bottom of this."

* * * * * *

Sloan and Perez, followed by a flotilla of armed officers and members of the S.W.A.T. team, barged up into the gallery, with Max Horton bringing up the rear. Sloan directed the officers to disperse throughout the gallery, reconnoitering the area in turn for clues or any sign of the creature possibly hiding nearby.

"Jeez, what went on here?" Sloan said upon seeing the carnage wrought and the many wounded and distraught forms before him.

Latham looked up at him with an inimical look one could not easily forget. "Some psycho blew in here and killed people!"

"Paramedics are on the way," Sloan said before noticing the bloody, protoplasmic mass on the floor. He was stunned, raised his cap and ruffled his hair.

Latham must have noticed him staring at the goop, because he said, "One of the security guards. That thing did that to him."

"Holy..." Sloan said.

"It's no use, officers," Paul said, joining Latham and Sloan near the center of the promenade. "Whatever that was, it's gone."

Latham turned and cast him a strong glance. "That was mighty brave of you back there. I can't thank you enough."

"Robert, it was nothing," Paul said, appearing almost sheepish. He looked around. "Where's the commissioner?"

Sloan roused himself, and started to frantically search among the debris for any sign of his boss. "Perez, over here," he eventually cried out.

There, amongst small pieces of concrete and marble, lay Commissioner Harrison. He was unconscious, and there was a large, open gash on his forehead, now more exposed with the loss of his hairpiece. Otherwise, he appeared unharmed.

"He's wounded. Give me a hand here," Sloan said to Perez, who began shifting some of the rubble away from Harrison.

Paul and Latham raced over and did likewise.

Sloan began brushing the dust off Harrison, who was only now beginning to regain consciousness.

"Wha—" Harrison started.

"Stay calm, sir," Perez said, kneeling beside her partner. "You've been hurt."

"I—I'm okay," Harrison said weakly. "What happened? I heard an explosion...then nothing."

Sloan stood, eyed both Latham and Paul. "What happened? I need answers, and I need them now." The detective moved over to them. "Gentleman, maybe you can enlighten me?"

* * * * * *

A hum buzzed through the thickness of the dark. Aztekoth moved through the darkened passage toward the noise with graceful ease, belying his immense size and shape. The only sound was the slowly-building din of rhythmic chanting, seemingly coming from everywhere and nowhere at the same time. Navigating the route, Aztekoth finally reached a grand doorway. He pushed it open with his bony hands. The creature entered into an expansive chamber, with a high timber ceiling, its walls decorated with Aztec carvings of their gods. Pottery, gold and silver ornaments, ceremonial cloths and jewelry adorned the place. The only light came from the burning torches strung sporadically along the walls on each side of the chamber.

Aztekoth was greeted by wild chanting from dozens of figures, the first pew of which contained ten creatures, all skeletal, each seemingly ready to cheer on their leader.

He made his way to the head of his flock, stood behind a podium and waited for silence.

Across from him, the skeletal monsters were outfitted in the traditional garb of the Aztec warrior—costumes of leather, cloth robes and feathered headdresses. None of their attire, though, could hide the gruesome sight of a bloody, human heart beating within their bony ribcages. The men standing in the pews behind these monstrous warriors were outfitted as their skeletal counterparts, and were distinctly Aztec Indian in appearance; their flat, obsidian-like eyes, their iron focus, truly defined them. All brandished a long, wooden spear, and a braided, circular wooden shield.

Aztekoth raised his arms and the chanting slowly began to die down. Two Aztec warriors appeared from parted curtains at Aztekoth's rear and quickly made their way to stand either side of their leader.

"This city," Aztekoth began, "and Robert Latham in particular, have been made aware of their complicity in the desecration of our great artifact. Of our race." The creature's voice resonated in unworldly tones, exacerbated by the acoustics of the structure they were housed in. "This cannot be permitted to continue. And it will not!" The warriors cheered and chanted in unison. "The stone will soon be ours and therein also our salvation. With the bodies of this city's people, we will reform our long-dead empire, giving me the army I require. And once the stone has been retrieved, we will use it to give us true form—true *life*—once more!"

His words were met with thunderous applause and the chanting began anew with enhanced vigor. "Bring out the next sacrifice," it ordered.

The two nearest warriors swiftly vanished into the rear chamber, only to return mere moments later with a captive male.

Their victim, a man of average height and receding hairline, struggled against his tight bonds, but was harshly shaken into quiet compliance by the two, burly warriors. They dragged him over to Aztekoth and forced him to his knees before the monstrous cult leader.

Gagged, the victim could only mumble in terror.

"Do not fear me," Aztekoth said. "For it is your destiny to bestow the gift of life on one of our long-dead people. Your paltry existence will be given in sacrifice to restore those of our ancient warriors, cruelly taken from them by the infidel hordes from Spain and elsewhere. Now...rise!"

Aztekoth's eyes began to glow like the embers of a dying campfire, though with a hue so spectral, so sickeningly strobing as to have an hypnotic effect on the bound man. He stood as he was told, no longer shaking with fear.

"Accept your fate, find solace in the glory of the resurrected Aztec empire," Aztekoth said. He pointed to a wooden altar to his right at the furthest edge of the podium. The wretched victim blankly followed Aztekoth's directions, stopping once he reached it. Aztekoth and his two guards followed eagerly, then positioned the victim horizontally on the altar, fastening him in place with a series of leather straps. The hapless man looked up with an expression so emotionless he appeared almost lifeless.

"It is time to raise one of our vaunted few from their hallowed exile," Aztekoth thundered.

The creature produced an obsidian-made knife from the folds of his tattered robes and held it aloft for all to see. Intense chanting ensued as he plunged the knife into the chest of his victim. The helpless man made no sound or movement.

"To appease Huitzilopochtli, to ensure the rise of the sun, a heart must be procured," Aztekoth moaned.

Blood spurted from the victim's chest, gushing out onto the altar. Aztekoth continued ripping into him, his ribcage offering no barrier. Bones snapped; blood flowed. "And to raise the dead, it must be secured!" After more bone-crunching effort, he triumphantly raised the dripping, still-beating heart, above his head and was met with a deafening explosion of rhythmic chanting.

Aztekoth quickly moved down from the podium, over to a large wooden crate at the far end of the podium. With the beating heart in one hand, he lifted the lid off the crate with the other, revealing a primeval skeletal form covered with centuries' worth of dirt and grime. He reached down and carefully placed the heart on top of the skeleton's ribcage.

His arms raised above his head, he said, "Great Huitzilopochtli, accept this sacrifice as our way of appeasement. Grant us the gift of life once again!"

For some moments, nothing. Silence. Then, the heart still beating, began to seep through the ribs of the long dead Aztec warrior before solidifying again in the space where the warrior's own heart once beat. In seconds that seemed to go on forever, everyone remained silent and still. Suddenly, the skeleton began to shift, murmur ever so slightly within its narrow confines. Its fingers moved slowly, carefully, as though it was testing if it was still capable of movement after the many hundreds of years at rest. The chanting began again, quickly reaching fever pitch, as the skeleton's arms began to move. It then positioned its fingers and arms to lift itself from the crate. As it sat upright, it came into the view of the gathered flock, which only served to increase the tempo of their unified chanting.

"Behold, our great god has granted the gift of life once again," Aztekoth shrieked.

The skeletal warrior rose to its feet, its new heart beating within its bony shell. The two Aztec Indians bestowed upon it a wooden shield and spear and escorted it to join its brethren. The gathered cult now began to beat the end of their spears on the timber floor in conjunction with their continued chanting prayers.

"Soon we will have resurrected our entire cache of warriors. And then...then we resurrect the glory of the Aztec Empire here in America!" Aztekoth took a step closer toward its brethren. "In Metro City!"

~ Chapter 4 ~

It was morning, and while a weak sun managed to penetrate through the thick haze of a usually polluted and cloudy Metro City skyline, the rain had, momentarily, relented. Commissioner George Harrison and Detective's Bob Sloan and Rosa Perez were crammed into Harrison's small and cramped office. Harrison, despite receiving a mild concussion the night before, arrived at work before everyone else—as per usual—which could not fail to impress Sloan, though he expected nothing less from the man.

"Commissioner, are you sure you should be in today?" Perez asked, looking concerned.

Harrison fired her a hard look, which Sloan had also expected but he could not help himself from exhibiting a wry smile. He looked at Perez, who was working hard to contain a slight grin from escalating into something more. Sloan looked at Harrison's bald pate and felt the same urge for laughter but managed to keep it under control.

"The mayor's already had a word with me this morning. With the election coming up, he's worried this city's finest will withdraw their support if something isn't done fast. So, I want to go over again what happened last night." He was clearly determined to ascertain exactly what happened the night previous and to capture those responsible.

Sloan pulled from his pocket a small notepad and flipped it open. "Sometime around 10 P.M., immediately after the unveiling of the Cortes Stone, an explosion ripped through the front entrance, injuring several of the guests, and—" Harrison now shot Sloan *that* look. Sloan raised his eyebrows before continuing. "Yes, well...some guy wearing tattered rags appeared and proceeded to tear up the place, killing one of the guards and threatening the guests, singling out Robert Latham in particular. He seems to have some connection to the stone and/or the Aztecs. Called itself Aztekoth."

Sloan slapped his notepad shut and glanced at his partner then at the commissioner. Perez seemed to be going over the details in her mind. Harrison appeared to be replaying to himself what Sloan had just said, as if making sure he got it right.

The commissioner broke the silence. "This...Aztekoth. You say it killed a guard. I saw the guard's...remains...last night. How could a man do something like that to another human being?"

Perez appeared downcast. "I—I don't know. It's not possible, obviously...and yet..."

"No, I refuse to believe it," Sloan said. "You're right, it's *not* possible. There's some trick to it, obviously. Maybe the guests were hallucinating? There were reports of smoke emanating from Aztekoth's body somehow. Maybe that acted as some sort of a hallucinogen?"

Harrison's face lit up a little at this. "That's a good point, Detective. There are no doubt several options which I'd believe before taking those eyewitness accounts at face value. And yet we have the guard's body in that...state...to prove otherwise. I suggest that's where we take this next: examine those options a little closer and determine just how this freak pulled it off. I won't allow these kinds of attacks to continue." Harrison flopped into the under-sized leather chair behind his over-cluttered desk.

"Right," Sloan said to Perez, as she exited Harrison's office en route to her own desk.

Sloan stayed behind briefly, removed something from his pocket. "Here you go, Commissioner. I rescued this last night." It was his boss's hairpiece. Harrison shot him *that* look again and pointed to the door. Sloan smiled and briefly thought of saying something smart, but ultimately thought better of it.

He left the commissioner's office.

"Let's start with the hallucinogen angle," Sloan said, joining Perez at her desk. "Something tells me that's our best bet at this stage. I suggest we have a little talk with Howard before anything else. I want to know more about hallucinogenic drugs and if it's possible that it might have been used last night."

"But the guard's body?"

He gave no reply.

"And then?" Perez sighed.

"Then I think we need to re-interview some of last night's guests—Robert Latham and Paul Sanderson specifically."

* * * * * *

The expanse of The Wraith's Lair stretched out around Paul who, along with Leena and Max, paced within its confines. The Lair was a massive, unique architectural structure comprising two levels. Its entry was achieved via a hidden doorway located in the Sanderson House study library, out onto the upper storey of the Lair, which wrapped around its outer edge like a protective corset and which housed their costumes and other equipment. A small, circular elevator brought one down to the lower level, where The Wraith's computer terminals, communications portal, laboratory, gymnasium and electronics workshop were located. Though the size and shape of a limestone cavern akin to Carlsbad, the Lair looked anything but. Its walls were metallic and shiny, very 1930s Art Deco in style, but also a mix of the modern, and in stark contrast to the Victoria Era appearance of the house above.

Paul continued pacing, while noting that both Leena and Max had stopped and were now staring at him. It was Paul who finally broke the silence.

"I cannot reconcile what I saw with what I know to be true," he said. "And yet..."

"It's hard for me to believe as well, Chief, but...we have come across enemies before with strange abilities that cannot be explained by modern science," Max said.

Leena looked perplexed and somewhat concerned. "We all heard over the transmitter in Commissioner Harrison's office the theory the police seem to think most valid." She faced Paul. "Could we have been exposed to such a hallucinogen?"

"Impossible. We would have felt its effects this morning, and no matter how real such a hallucination may have appeared to me at the time, *I* would have known had my senses been altered such. No, as hard as it is to believe, what we saw *was* real." He paused, scowled. "How can we fight something like this?"

The team could find no answers then, but despite the incredible evil that had newly surfaced, Paul knew they would fight, struggle, until the enemy had been defeated—or they'd die in the attempt.

Leena peeked at her Tissot watch, and suddenly came to life. "I have to go, darling, I'm late for work. It won't do to miss another day; I've missed too many as it is."

Paul acknowledged her. His love for her knew no bounds, and he knew it was important to conduct their civilian lives as normally and best they could even in the midst of such an emerging malevolent force as Aztekoth. "Of course. Max and I will continue with the job at hand."

The soft humming of the doorway to the Lair signaled the entry of the Sanderson butler Jonathan Simpson, a tall, taciturn man with graying hair and piercing eyes. He appeared at the upper level's edge.

"I have taken the liberty of arranging a small breakfast, Miss," Simpson said. He presented her with a wrapped bagel. "Your favorite on-the-go morning meal."

Leena smiled, kissed Paul farewell, leaped into the elevator and was soon by the butler's side. "Thanks." She took a large bite. "What would we do without you, Simpson?"

"I shudder to imagine."

The two retreated from the Lair, slipping through the secret entrance.

Paul turned to face Max. "Get in touch with all our contacts. There must be information out there."

The two hunkered down at the Lair's communication's portal, intent on getting the answers they needed.

* * * * * *

Latham slammed his fist onto his desk. "Nobody threatens me, least of all at one of my own functions in front of this city's elite!"

Charlie Grieco seemed non-plussed by his superior's ravings.

While Latham sat at his desk, Grieco maneuvered around and alongside the various busts Latham had collected throughout his ornately decorated study, busts of the great dictators throughout history that Latham revered. His boss had often told him that these leaders shared with him much of the qualities he admired. The young capo glanced intermittently at them while Latham spoke.

"Whoever these people are, I want you to find them, Charlie, and punish them. No one does this to me and gets away with it. The word has to get out that they were dealt with and dealt with quickly. Nothing else will do. And make sure the stone is now guarded with the utmost security. Is that understood?"

"Yes, Mr. Latham," Grieco said blankly. He knew it was futile to argue or even offer an opinion when his boss was in such a mood. It would only be shot down no matter what was said. He had to remain cautious. His thirst for power remained; indeed it was as strong as ever, but now was not the time to exercise it. He had plans in place, plans that percolated like his favorite cappuccino, but patience was still required. He would wait for the right moment.

* * * * * *

It had been a hectic morning at the Metro City Public Library, one of the busiest libraries in the state, and Leena was still tired from the late hour of the previous night. She plopped down onto her chair at her desk in the back staffroom, ready to gulp down her first cup of coffee for the day. Morning break didn't come soon enough, and she was ready to enjoy this brief respite.

"Doesn't get any easier, does it?" Janet, a new colleague of Leena's at the library with whom she had become a fast friend, said in passing.

Leena smiled. "Typical Monday."

"Well, don't get too comfy. You're back out there in fifteen minutes."

"Don't remind me," she groaned, rolling her eyes.

She picked up the framed photo of Paul on her desk and lovingly ran a finger along his face. It was sometimes hard to believe the life she was now living: girlfriend and partner to Paul Sanderson, the former reclusive multi-millionaire of Metro City. More than that, she was the partner of The Wraith Dread Avenger of the Underworld, a man who had sworn his life to justice, and who had been responsible time and again for the salvation, not only of the city, but, indeed, the entire nation. Somehow, the life of Sanderson had become intertwined with that of her boyfriend Michael Reeve, and the two had become one in a way she still didn't quite understand. What she *did* understand, only too well, was that she had lost him once and would never go through that again. Once she discovered what had happened—and realized what she'd lost—she refused to leave him She then had to endure a taxing training regime to be able to live, love and fight by his side. She did not doubt for a moment that she could never love anyone as much as she did Paul. Ever.

Janet passed by again, stirring Leena from her ruminating. "Leena, you're meant to be back on the desk."

"I'm sorry, Janet. I was just...thinking. I'll be right out."

Leena smiled as she placed the photo back on her desk then rushed out to attend to her next shift on the library reference desk.

Time passed slowly. What started as a regular two hour shift turned into a double-shift (a temporary staff member called in sick, and Leena thought it best if she just continued manning the desk as she'd done all morning). As well as the usual loans—for she found herself needed on the circulation desk almost as often as the reference desk—there were innumerable queries on subjects ranging from the original peoples of Siberia to the myriad gemstones of Africa. Finally, during a lull in the afternoon, she was able to see to the shelving, and helped her colleagues in that often onerous task.

Down in the reference section, while tidying amongst the encyclopedias and dictionaries, her ears perked up at the exchange going on nearby. She pushed aside two thick monographs and peered through to the other side. There, two sturdy men were seated at a table, carefully examining what looked like a detailed plan.

But a plan of what? She strained to hear what the men were saying.

"Are we all set for tonight?" the man on the right said. Leena estimated he was in his twenties given his spiky brown hair and his disheveled and dusty-looking leather jacket.

"I think so," the other man said. He was older, much more course and harsher-looking in his visage, and had much less hair. Judging from the tone of his voice, the manner of his speech, Leena guessed he was the leader of the two. "These old plans from the library here show us exactly where the stash is, based on Malone's diaries."

Malone's diaries, she thought.

"3 A.M. then. Dave's joining us, right? He ain't chickening out?" the younger man said.

"I won't let 'im."

Leena waited a moment longer, but the men had become silent, and she couldn't neglect her duties for too long. She rounded the shelf and made her way back toward the reference desk, past the two men with their plan still unfurled on the table. The elder man eyed her suspiciously through squinting eyes as she passed them and returned to her post.

The afternoon dragged on like so many others. Leena's thoughts drifted from that of the conversation she'd overheard back to the night before, to Aztekoth and the horrors of the City Gallery. She'd seen much in her time as partner to the Dread Avenger of the Underworld, but nothing could compare with the terror she'd felt when that Grim Reaper-like monster moved ominously toward them. She shuddered briefly, tried shrugging the feeling off.

Leena glanced at her watch. 4:30P.M. *Good. Nearly time to go home.*

She breathed heavily, mentally readying herself for the rush hour trip home. She smiled as several patrons passed her and exited the library.

The two men from earlier came toward her. She smiled at them as well but then quickly furled her brow when the elder of the two said, "Take care of this, will ya?" and tossed the plan at her as they marched from the library.

How rude, Leena thought.

She scooped the plan up and intended to return it to the archives area in the reference department, but curiosity got the better of her and she decided to take a peak at what they were researching. Unfurling the plan, her eyes widened at the name emblazoned near the top.

"Stanton Station," she said under her breath. The name struck an instant chord in her memory, particularly in light of the previous mention of Malone's diaries. She had to alert Paul to the significance of this as quickly as possible. Thankfully, business had trailed off since the morning, and she was able to have a colleague watch the desk for a few moments so she could duck into the staffroom.

Locking herself into a bathroom cubicle, Leena opened her purse and pulled out a compact. She opened it. Inside, amongst an intricate mixture of electronics and wiring, was a small earpiece. She took it and placed it into her ear. She then held the compact up before her mouth.

"Darling, come in," she whispered.

"Yes, Leena," came Paul's reply a few moments later.

"Paul...some men in the library were viewing the plans of Stanton Station, and they mentioned Malone's diaries."

There was a pause before he said, "Understood. We'll be ready once you return from work. Good job. Paul out."

She smiled. It would soon be time to leave for the day, and then her *other* job would begin.

* * * * * *

In the Lair, Paul placed the headphone back in its cradle.

"Malone's diaries you say?" Max enquired. "You think so?"

Paul turned in his chair to face the burly Irishman.

"Sounds like it," He stood. "We'll know soon enough."

Paul, mind racing, moved over to the stairwell leading up the promenade where a host of Wraith costumes were stored and went up the steps.

Karl Malone had been a petty thief, drug dealer, car-jacker and innumerable other things in his lifetime. What he'd actually acquired fame for was, perhaps, the most audacious theft Metro City had ever seen. He and his gang had made off with legitimate plates for printing five dollar bills. In essence, Malone could print as much money as he could ever hope to want, and they would not be forgeries in the true sense, but indistinguishable from proper currency. And by printing only five dollar bills, he could use them at will very discreetly instead of drawing attention to himself by flashing around a plethora of fifties or hundreds. Malone was eventually caught, but no trace of the plates were ever found, and nothing or nobody could make Malone reveal what he'd done with them.

Had he just hidden them away somewhere? Paul thought. *Had he actually printed some bills already, and hidden those too? Or–?*

Paul removed one of his cowls from its stand and stared at it briefly. Peering into the eyeholes, it was almost as though he was staring into the soul of another, and for the briefest of moments, a strange feeling came over him. Not being able to explain it, the feeling passed and he merely shrugged it off. He would get to the bottom of the Malone mystery tonight, but he also knew that his attention was required elsewhere: toward the serial killings bedeviling his city, and toward the creature Aztekoth. So far that night, both he and Max had turned up nothing on that front. None of their contacts knew a thing about the creature. He promised there and then to make quick work of the Malone conundrum, and turn his mind and energies back to where they were really needed.

~ Chapter 5 ~

Night was beginning to fall, and it was then that Metro City took on a whole new countenance. During the day, the city was pleasant enough. Somewhat downtrodden and neglected in places, as most large cities were, but Robert Latham and certain newly-elected civic officials had done much to beautify portions of the city, just enough to bring a definite spark back into those areas that had seen such refurbishment. But only during the day. At night, the cities lowlifes and scum would re-appear from their hiding places, and Metro would appear as it always had, a cesspool at war with itself.

Detectives Sloan and Perez and Commissioner Harrison were gathered in a narrow, putrid alley on Metro's west-side, along with several other police officers and C.S.I. technicians. Another body was discovered tonight, and Sloan could only lift his baseball cap and scratch his head at the awful sight now before him. On the ground lay an average-sized man of close to middle age, with a receding hairline. What made him stand out, however, were the terrible wounds on his torso. Blood was strewn all around and it was clear that his ribs had been ripped open and the heart removed. It was nowhere to be seen.

"According to his license, this is Richard Stanley, forty three years old, address in Gladstone Heights," Perez said.

Sloan knelt beside her. "Poor guy. His heart missing, like all the others. Who could be responsible for this?" He stood and faced the nearest C.S.I. officer. "You got anything?"

"We're still going through certain pieces of evidence," the officer replied, "but I doubt we'll get anything substantial. As with the previous victims, there have been no fingerprints left, nothing to identify the perpetrators. We do have this, however." He held aloft an evidence bag which contained a small, tan piece of rag.

"Hmm..." Sloan breathed, examining the piece of material. "Could finally be something to go on."

"Get this to the lab, I want answers as quickly as possible," Harrison barked. "And get the body over to the morgue. I want Boynce's autopsy report on my desk by morning."

As the C.S.I. officers carefully bagged the body, Sloan, Perez and Harrison stepped to the side of the scene.

"This must be the result of a satanic cult. The organs haven't been sold on the black market, that much we've been able to ascertain recently," Perez said.

"I don't know. I just—" Sloan said.

"What, Bob?" Perez asked. "You're not convinced?"

"I don't know. I can't put my finger on it. I agree, on the face of it, the satanic cult angle is a convincing one. And yet..." His voice trailed off.

Sloan rubbed his chin and separated from his colleagues, absentmindedly shuffling up the trash-strewn alley. He turned back to face them.

"I'm just not ready to concede the point. I still feel there's something more to this, something even more terrible than some kind of a satanic cult behind all this. And I'm going to find out what it is."

He stormed from the alley with a purposeful stride and could hear Perez's footfalls behind him. Being partners for as long as they had been, he knew her step—indeed everything about her—better than anyone else. He also knew that she would follow him to the gates of Hell in search of answers to these horrible crimes.

He wasn't about to let her down now.

* * * * * *

Leena pulled her coat up over her neck as she made her way to her car in its usual spot in the library parking lot. It had just started to drizzle and the rain brought with it the first northerly, chill wind of the season. As she neared her Mini, she thought she caught the sound of footsteps behind her.

Another staff member, she thought, but she briefly had this odd feeling that she was being followed. It was a feeling she didn't like and a feeling she always heeded. She turned...

No one there.

Odd.

Upon reaching her car, she got in, started it and pointed it out into the street. As she began to turn into the side-alley leading to the main thoroughfare, a four by four appeared as though from nowhere and careened into the side of the Mini, causing the side and curtain airbags to burst to life and sent the car skidding up onto the sidewalk. Before she could even react, two men were at her car's side, pulling her from it and tossing her into the back of their truck.

Paralyzed temporarily with shock, she decided to bide her time. She needed to calm down first, needed to regain her composure and her wits before doing anything else. And she needed to know what these people were up to. Lying uncomfortably in amongst a selection of tools, Leena blocked out the pain. She would wait, feigning unconsciousness...to listen and learn.

* * * * * *

Robert Latham sat hunched over his desk at home, working late, signing various documents requiring his signature. He often worked from this large office at home, sometimes preferring it to his office at Latham Industries in the city which felt to him, despite it being *his* office in *his* building, somewhat stuffy and stilted. Here, at home, he could revel in his surroundings, delight in his good taste, and perhaps let his mind wander ever so briefly from time-to-time from the burdens of running an empire such as his. Not that he ever let his mind wander too far from the business at hand. Latham was too consummate a professional to ever let his guard down for more than an instant. No. But at home he was able to use the busts of the dictators he so admired surrounding him to inspire him. The power these figures of history wielded was a power such Latham could only dream of, despite his lofty position within the city. He dreamed of wielding such power on an ever grander scale, and had the confidence within himself to think—nay, to *know*—he could achieve such.

While Latham smiled at the thought of increasing his power-base, Charlie Grieco entered the study, manila folder in hand.

"Everything signed, Mr. Latham?" the deputy said.

"Yes, yes," he replied, somewhat shortly. "Have your investigations thus far borne fruit?"

Grieco looked a little ill-at-ease at this question and fidgeted with his tie as a result. "Not yet, but I have my boys tracking down leads. It's only a matter of time before those behind all this will be hunted down and eliminated."

Latham could feel the hair on the back of his neck stand on end. He bristled at the lack of progress in finding Aztekoth, or those behind the creature, and punishing them. If there was one thing he prized dearly, it was efficiency. As he saw it, if he could be efficient in everything he did, then there was no reason why others, especially those he employed, could not be likewise, no matter the circumstances. However, he contained his emotions somewhat before replying.

"I see," he started, before pausing. "I take it you are continuing to oversee this operation personally?"

Grieco squirmed. Latham often delighted in making him feel uncomfortable, thinking it best to never allow his power-hungry deputy to feel too comfortable in his position within the organization. The way he saw it, if Grieco were always kept on edge, his position always appearing to him tenuous at best, then his deputy would be easier to handle and to kept on-leash. This would help allay any doubts Grieco may have as to who is truly in charge and prevent him from ever even contemplating a challenge against his authority. To do so would be sheer suicide.

"Yes, definitely. I'm handling every aspect of this operation from the ground up," Grieco said.

Latham stood, but remained passive behind his immense desk. "Then perhaps you should be out there *handling it* rather than collecting my signed documents?" There was some menace in that statement, and Latham could see by Grieco's expression that the message had been received and understood.

His deputy nodded meekly in agreement and made his way for the exit.

Latham reached for the beautifully enameled bronze cigar box on his desk and procured a sizable specimen from it. He removed the band, carefully snipped the tip and lit it with a bejeweled lighter. He sauntered over to the large bay window behind him and blew smoke rings while looking out into the night. The lights of the city sparkled out from beyond his estate, serving a reminder of the empire—*his empire*—close to hand. The view always gave him a feeling of satisfaction, knowing that all that before him was his. And the city *was* his, there was never any doubt of this, and he would let no man counter his way of thinking in that matter.

There was nothing else for it. Most of the documents requiring his signature had been signed, but there were other issues requiring his attention, and he'd turned his attention from those for too long as it was. Taking one last look at the city, he turned and made his way slowly back to his desk. Before he had moved two steps, however, he heard an eerie sound coming from his rear, from the window where he had only moments before stood.

He normally prided himself on his strength of character, on his courage, but the sound, akin to that of fingernails being run across a blackboard sent shivers down his spine. Despite this feeling, he turned.

There, on the other side of the window, stood Aztekoth, its bony hand raised, its eyes glowering a sickening shade of crimson.

Latham gasped without meaning to.

The creature simply stood there, statue-like, and Latham similarly remained rooted to the spot, frozen with fear, unable to decide his next course of action.

"Robert Latham!" the creature suddenly droned.

"You have sinned against the gods. The greatness of the Aztec Empire is ready to rise once more, and your evil will not be allowed to hinder our progress."

Those icy words cut deep into his psyche. It was clear the creature blamed him for something.

But what? The acquisition of the stone?

Latham, regaining his composure somewhat, rushed over to an intercom system located on the sideboard to his right.

"Get in here. Now!" Latham barked. The order completed, he returned his gaze toward the bay window to find the creature now stood on his side of the glass inside the study.

Aztekoth floated along the floor toward him. Latham gasped again then quickly snapped his mouth shut. While he did have some measure of pride in what he perceived as his own courage under fire, he could no longer bite back the terror the creature had undoubtedly intended to inflict upon him. As the creature advanced, Latham stumbled backward, lurched against the sideboard, desperate for escape. His breathing became labored, sweat began pouring from his brow, and he struggled along the length of the sideboard, vainly trying to make it to the door, his feet seemingly made of clay.

Aztekoth continued advancing, emotionless, ominous.

"There is no escape for such as you," the creature said. "Your treachery cannot go unpunished." The thing was nearly upon him.

Latham caught his foot on the corner of his exquisite Persian rug and collapsed in a heap before the door he had fought so hard to reach.

"Your life will be sacrificed for a worthy cause," Aztekoth said, looming in front of him. "Your time on this planet is now at an end!"

In that instant, a complete change came over Latham, his demeanor going from one extreme to the next. He had heard the footfalls of his approaching men. He looked up and smiled at the creature.

"Not this time," he said, and rolled out of the line of fire.

Instantly, the door burst open, four men appearing, guns raised and firing directly at the creature. Aztekoth was flung back under the barrage of bullets. It made no noise, there was no visible sign of pain or injury, but the creature had fallen.

Latham was quick to his feet, and walked tentatively over to view the monster's body.

"Never underestimate me, creature," Latham said. "Many have. All have failed."

The creature made no sound or movement. Latham kicked at the filthy pile of rags on the floor.

The body was gone.

One of the men whistled in amazement.

Latham crouched down by the side of the rags, ruffled his hair, breathed heavily. He wasn't sure what had just happened, but even he knew what a lucky escape he'd just had. And that fact troubled him.

Greatly.

~ Chapter 6 ~

The Wraith scanned the city from the roof of the Latham Industries building, the tallest structure in Metro City, the perfect vantage point. A slight breeze had picked up and caused his cape to flutter about him, as he drew his night-vision binoculars from one side of the city to the other in search of prey. He hadn't heard from Leena since earlier that day and she hadn't returned home from work at her usual time either. While he wasn't worried—she was too well trained for that—he nevertheless had a strange feeling rising from the pit of his stomach.

Has she gone off on her own investigation? Has she been discovered and taken captive?

These questions and more rattled around his brain, but rather than wait at home he thought it best to get an early start on his nightly patrols before potentially investigating Leena's absence and, of course, the Malone diaries.

He turned his mind over to other matters. Night had only just fallen, so there was still time for Leena to let him know what the situation currently was. If he knew his girl, she had somehow bitten off more than she could chew. He smiled briefly. He also knew that that applied to anyone who had gotten on her bad side, and if it was anyone involved with the Malone diaries he knew they'd be in all sorts of trouble before they knew what hit them.

Movement. From the alley below. At first he thought nothing of it. It was a public space, after all, and he would expect there to be people milling about, especially at night in Metro City. Even so, with all that had been happening, he thought it better to investigate further. He pressed a button to the right side of the binoculars, zooming in on street level. As he did, the infra-red vision kicked in and the darkened alley instantly lit up a bright green.

Coming into view were a band of walking skeletons, spears and shields in tow, trudging down the alleyway.

The Wraith placed the binoculars in a pouch on his belt then withdrew his grapnel and line. He fired it upward, the grappling hook catching on the radio tower at the peak of the Latham building and gently lowered himself down.

* * * * * *

As the truck came to a screeching halt, Leena found herself yanked harshly from the back of it and a tight hood pulled over her head before she had time to react. She said nothing, remaining compliant, waiting to properly discern their plans and their location. She hadn't any idea yet of either, but planned to find out as soon as possible.

"C'mon, get moving," came the voice she recognized as the leader of the duo from the library earlier that day. She received a rough shove in her back. Again, she complied and walked forward.

After a minute or so, and entering some kind of structure, she was told to sit down. Her hood was removed. She spluttered, eager to put on the act of innocence, and allowed herself a few moments for her eyes to adjust to the light shining in her face.

"Where am I? What do you want from me?" she cried, playing it up a little. Now she could make out the two men from the library standing before her, confirming her earlier thoughts. The leader of the two flashed her a lascivious grin.

"You were listening in on our conversation," he said. "You heard too much."

"I don't know what you're talking about. I heard nothing," she replied.

"Don't give me that," the leader said, bending forward, his face inches from hers. "You saw the plans. You spied on us through the book shelves."

"None of that meant anything to me, I swear," Leena whimpered, laying the act on thick for her captors. Little did they know just what they'd gotten themselves into.

The younger of the two grabbed the elder by the arm. "Hey, she doesn't know anything. I told ya this was a waste of time."

The leader pulled his arm free. "We couldn't take any chances, not with everything that we have at stake." He bent forward, pressed his face into hers. He gritted his teeth and she could smell the fowl stench of stale beer and bad takeout. "You just sit there nice and quiet and everything will be fine."

He took a step back and paused briefly before saying to his partner, "Keep a watch on her. I'll be in the office, waiting for Dave."

The leader stalked off behind her and out of view. She heard a door slam and she was left facing the young man, who fidgeted about in his chair.

She took a moment to get her bearings, at least in regards to the interior of her current surrounds. She looked above and around. She was in an abandoned warehouse, that much was obvious, probably on or near the waterfront from the look and smell of things. Dust and cobweb-strewn timber arches and pylons stretched out above her, culminating in a V-shaped roof. Shabby crates of every size and shape were on all sides, with one crate beneath her. The only door she could perceive was likely the door she had come in only a few minutes earlier. The air was filled with a musty odor and she felt sure she could also smell the sea, thus confirming they were indeed on or near the waterfront.

She turned her attention back toward the man guarding her. He fidgeted with his wallet and belt buckle, appearing almost desperate for something to do aside from what he was meant to be doing.

"Please let me go," she pleaded. "I don't know anything, I swear."

The young man's appearance suggested he seemed to believe her. "Look, it wasn't my idea to bring you here. But there's nothing I can do. Nick would kill me if he even knew we were talking like this."

Nick, eh? Leena thought. *And Dave. Perhaps I can learn more.*

"What's this all about? I just want to go home. You don't need me here for whatever you have planned."

The man put his finger to his lips, as though shushing her. "I can't talk, you know I can't. Just sit back and take it easy for now."

"Will you let me go? I can't be of any help to you. I really don't know anything about all this."

The man looked furtively around. "Why won't you just be quiet?"

Leena acted as though she was about to start crying.

"Please, just be quiet," he said, trying his best to calm her down. "Look, as soon as we collect the stash, we'll let you go, I swear. Just hang in there and everything will be fine."

As if, she thought. *There's no way Nick will let me go, at least not alive.*

But she was making some progress, and if she was able to press for further details, there was hope she could wrap this up fairly easily.

"What's your name?" she asked.

The man suddenly appeared very ill-at-ease at this and continued to wriggle in his seat, but he eventually supplied a stammering answer. "Ed...Eddie. The name's Eddie."

"Eddie..." Leena began, but was cut off with the appearance of another man at the doorway. He casually made his way toward them, a shorter man of around the same age as Eddie, and just as disheveled in appearance, but with longer, albeit stringy hair and wearing a torn sweater and jeans.

This must be Dave, she thought.

"Who's the chick?" he said matter-of-factly.

Before Eddie had a chance to reply, Nick stormed out from his office and greeted Dave with a snarl.

"About time you showed up here."

"Hey, I told you I'd make it," Dave said. "We got plenty of time anyway."

Nick grabbed Dave by the collar. "I want to go over the plan one last time, and we need to get the equipment ready. We have plenty to do before we're ready to go."

Dave gulped. "S—sure. Okay."

Nick indicated to Dave to head for the rear office before facing Eddie. "Tie her up. We need you back here to go over things."

Eddie found some nearby rope and did as he was told. Leena noted the weak knots, knowing full well she could make her escape with ease at any instant. But that would potentially cause the gang to give up their quest, at least for now, and she would never learn the location of the plates. Apprehending these thugs now would yield a couple of kidnappers, but would leave the bigger prize undiscovered. No, she wasn't in any immediate danger, she determined, so she would continue to bide her time, and wait. And learn.

* * * * * *

As the troop of skeletons, ten in total, trudged onward through the murky depths of the alleyway, The Wraith followed at a discreet distance. His in-cowl night-vision lenses in place, every movement of the eerie army ahead of him was clear. These guys definitely belonged to Aztekoth, but what their evil plans were he knew not.

Perhaps returning to their den? Whatever their aim or their course, he would follow them.

For several blocks, the army of the undead continued their path through the gloomy din before finally entering a more dingy part of the city where the surrounding buildings were more run-down, and the shadows cast an ever-lengthening melancholy. The rain began to fall once more, casting the creatures in a further pall. The Wraith had to be careful lest his footfalls give away his position. The way was slow-going, for the skeletons were clearly aware of their need to remain in the darkness and out of sight.

He followed this grotesque coterie for what seemed like hours, but for what ultimately amounted to little more than forty minutes of trudging through a harsh Metro City downpour. At the entry to one of Metro's innumerable alleyways The Wraith stopped and carefully peered around the corner of a decrepit tenement building. He was just able to make out the last few skeletons darting around another corner at the alley's furthest point. Carefully, he moved from his vantage point, down the narrow alley and reached the next corner swiftly. Proceeding with caution, he attempted to ascertain the progress of the skeletal warriors.

They were gone.

~ Chapter 7 ~

The Wraith stood there, unable to fathom just what had happened. Then he stirred himself.

Pull yourself together, man, he thought. *They obviously went somewhere.*

He bit his lip, furrowed his brow. He wasn't prepared to admit defeat, that they had escaped him. Not quite yet. Nothing was coming in on his built-in infra-red scope. He tapped at his cowl's left temple, switching the infra-red off. There was some light emanating from the surrounding buildings, as well as from a nearby lamppost, but there was no sign of the skeletal warriors.

He skirted along the surrounding walls, searching for any hidden doorways. There were none. Not perturbed, he moved over to the wall in front of him, aiming to again skim his hands along the wall's surface, searching for any possible way through. As he attempted to place his hands on the crumbling bricked surface of the wall, they melted through it, as though the wall were made of water.

The Wraith took a step back to briefly gather his wits.

What is *this?* he thought.

He reached out and again allowed his hand, his arm, to seep through what, to his eyes, looked as much like a regular brick wall as the others surrounding him. A wave of nausea enveloped him, until he pulled his arm free and the feeling passed. The image of the wall moved about like the surface of a still pond being slightly disturbed by a pebble thrown in by an eager child.

A hologram? Has to be, though I've never encountered something on this scale before. The technology at play here must be staggering.

He'd tarried enough. Without another thought, he took a large step and walked straight through the pseudo-wall. On the other side was merely the continuation of the alley.

Strange, he thought. *Surely I'd remember this alley?* He'd made a special note of most of the streets and alleys of this part of the city long ago, and his lack of knowledge of what was currently transpiring here surprised, even troubled, him. But he had no time for such personal recriminations. He had to push on.

Up ahead, despite the noise of the surrounding downpour, he thought he could just make out the sounds of hurried steps ahead of him through the ever-deepening puddles. He decided to risk it and began to run forward, trying to catch up to them and discover their purpose, if nothing else.

He kept to the outermost rim of the alley where the puddles were the least deep to keep the sound of his pursuit to an absolute minimum. He rounded a corner and just managed to catch sight of them through the haze of the current downpour.

The skeletons quickened their pace. Were they now aware of his presence? It didn't matter.

The Wraith picked up his pace, too, finding himself sprinting to keep up with their surprising speed. Rounding yet another corner, he ran into a somewhat wider, though deserted, cul-de-sac, just in time to catch the warriors darting into what appeared to be an empty warehouse. Its windows were heavily cracked, others completely shattered and its walls were stained with graffiti of the most virulent kind; a common sight in Metro City.

In moments, the Dread Avenger reached the warehouse, spotted the nearest window and tried to peer through. The glass was marked with years of grime and soot, making it impossible to see through. He made his way over to the door instead. He found it unlatched. That clinched it. No door was ever left unlocked in Metro, and he knew then that his presence *had* indeed been discovered, that some method of trap had now been laid for him. He pondered his next move carefully but quickly. There had to be another means of entry beside the immediate door and window. An upstairs window perhaps?

No, he thought. He would try the roof and hope for a possible entry there.

He pulled his grapnel gun from his belt, pointed it upwards and fired. The grappling hook shot out, expanded upon contact with the air, its attached line streaming behind it. The hook latched onto the roof and within seconds, he was yanked upward. A few seconds later, he sat hunched upon the warehouse roof, scanning the area.

A skylight.

The skeletons surely hadn't counted on this, he thought.

He carefully lifted the glass panel, and with little noise, pried it fully open and slipped inside. Dropping onto a slender catwalk with an easy grace, The Wraith silently stalked along its path in his eagerness to find the perfect vantage point. He soon found it, a spot where he could see the floor below but remain hidden from view. He settled there and waited. There was no sign of the walking skeletons.

Have they actually escaped? he could only hope not.

He scanned around for any sign of his quarry. It was dark, but there was enough light to see that the warehouse was largely empty, save for a few crates and a lot of dust and cobwebs. The skeletons were nowhere to be seen.

The Wraith mulled the situation over in his mind. There was nothing else for it. He couldn't remain up in the rafters much longer, lest the skeletons get too far of a head-start on him. Attaching his line to an overhead beam, he carefully lowered himself down to the warehouse floor.

Placing the grapnel and line back into his belt, he crouched down, searching for any evidence of the skeletons' path. Their footprints were evident in the thick dust, removing any doubt they had indeed entered the building.

But where are they?

He eyed the floor carefully, following their traces as best he might. The warehouse was large, the timber flooring ancient and of dubious condition, which made the going more precarious than it otherwise might have been.

The Wraith continued his hunt.

After some moments, the footprints ended at the farthest wall. He'd reached too many of those this night, and began to search for yet another secret entry. However, before he'd had a chance to check for any latches or buttons on the wall itself, the floor suddenly opened up beneath him.

He plummeted.

* * * * * *

Leena, bound, blindfolded and gagged, rattled about in the rear of the van she had been bundled into several minutes earlier. The van lurched over potted roads and turned innumerable times; enough to ensure she had no idea where they were.

They couldn't have left the city limits, she thought. *We haven't been driving that long.* That thought heartened her, though she knew she was in no real danger.

She'd seen and heard enough from her kidnappers to know they were strictly amateurs, at least in comparison with the likes of Robert Latham and some of the other foes she had faced in the past.

As she attempted to right herself, the van came to a sudden stop, sending her sprawling once again. An instant later, the van's rear door opened with a squeak and she was yanked out.

"Get outta there!" Nick barked.

She was pushed forward and led onward for a short distance outside before she heard the opening of a door and was directed inside. Once there, she heard the door being closed again. A second more and a bright light lit up through the fabric of her blindfold. Her blindfold was torn off and she made an act of being stunned and extremely frightened.

"Wh...where are we? What are you going to do with me?" she whimpered.

Nick glowered at her and pushed her forward once again. "Get going, we ain't got all night."

They were in a rundown tenement building, possibly abandoned by the looks of it; cobwebs weaved their intricate course throughout the narrow corridor they were in and the dirt and dust made breathing somewhat difficult. Still bound, the going was tough, particularly as Nick delighted in pushing and prodding her at every opportunity.

Rounding a corner, Leena spotted a door at the far end, which the rag-tag group headed for. Closer to it, the word *basement* became visible, as the group filed into the darkness one at a time. Flashlights snapped on simultaneously, and the staircase was illuminated in its wake. The gang proceeded downward, reaching the basement floor in reasonably quick time. The air was filled with a musty odor that caused Leena to almost gag. The smell of death hung in the air. Whether the inky blackness surrounding her contained the bodies of animals or some poor, wretched people, she didn't know.

After making their way through the darkened basement for some moments, illuminated only by their three flashlights, Nick stopped suddenly.

"This is the spot. Shine your lights here," he said.

The others did, and through the morass of dust and dirt, there appeared the faint outline of a trap door of some kind. Nick crouched down and rubbed some of the filth away with his palms.

"Yeah, this is it," he said again. "Hand me the crowbar. This thing won't budge."

Being covered in years' worth of grime, Leena wasn't surprised. Dave produced a small crowbar from his backpack and handed it to Nick, who then made quick work of the trap door.

"Jeez, this place is really hidden away," Eddie said.

"Naturally, or they woulda found it long ago," Nick replied.

Leena was ordered to proceed down first, and she continued complying with a quiet meekness befitting her implied image. As she tightly gripped the rusted, steel ladder, she glanced upward, and watched as Nick and the others quickly followed. The descent was a hazardous and lengthy one. Each rung appeared flimsier than the last, and the thickness of the rust began to bite into Leena's fingers. Down and down they went, further into a darkness the likes she had never experienced before. If not for her extensive training at the hands of the Dread Avenger of the Underworld, she might have felt a fear and loneliness in this place that could have crippled her. It took awhile, but she eventually reached bottom. She steadied herself, rubbing her now almost-raw hands. The others swiftly joined her, switching their lights back on.

Looking around her as best she could, she could see they were in a wide sewer tunnel, for the putrid smell of human waste was all around them.

This is certainly not Stanton Station, she thought.

"Let's go," Nick ordered once more. "This way."

They trudged through the shallow water at the center of the tunnel, where the going was easiest. Leena peered side-to-side. The tunnel was wide at its peak, but narrow at the base, forcing them to march through the rancid water. Further up, the floor and walls were covered in green slime.

As they continued their journey, the tunnel became increasingly narrower, clearly unnerving Eddie, who fidgeted about with enough fervor to prompt Nick to snap at him.

"Shut up back there! We're getting close."

Eddie calmed somewhat.

In this narrower section of tunnel, the air became heavier, the overriding feeling of oppression almost overwhelming. With the thin slivers of light shining their path forward, the group pressed on. Within minutes, they were forced to march single file, Leena behind Nick and Dave with Eddie bringing up the rear.

At last, Nick cried out. "We're here!"

Leena could hardly see where *here* was, unable to make much sense through the darkness and morass of heavy-set bodies in front of her. She could hear Nick scraping about the tunnel.

"Lemme see," Dave said impatiently.

He squeezed past Nick, allowing Leena some measure to see what the situation was for herself. They'd arrived at a dead end, but there was a small grate in the wall, much like a small, prison window (complete with bars), which seemed to captivate Nick and Dave.

"W—where are we?" Leena asked in a feigned shaky voice.

Nick ignored her, and the others merely followed suit.

"See it? Down there?" Nick pointed through the slender grate. "There it is."

Dave grunted in response, though she couldn't get close enough to the grate to make out just what the two thugs were talking about.

Stanton Station, it has to be, she thought.

"How are we gonna get down there?" Dave asked. "We have the rope, but how do we get through these bars?"

Leena was able to see Nick closely inspecting the bars themselves.

"They're pretty rusty. If we attach the rope to them and give a pull, we should be able to break through," Nick said.

"You won't be able to fit through the gap," Leena said, perhaps allowing too much of her real self to show through.

Nick barged past Dave and brought his face inches from hers. "We'll manage," he spat.

Leena was directed to take a few steps back, with Eddie watching her carefully, while Nick and Dave attached their ropes to the bars.

"Now, all of you, grab some rope and pull," Nick ordered.

They did and, despite the confines of their surroundings, tugged with all their might. With Leena's added strength, not that those thugs seemed to have any inkling of this, Nick had been right. The bars slowly began to give, first with a creak and cracking of steel and concrete, then with a sudden crashing of drywall on the tunnel floor, sending the gang tumbling into the shallow water.

"Holy crap! The tunnel's gonna cave in!" Eddie cried.

Leena smiled inwardly, though in truth she couldn't blame him for such a reaction. The noise of the bars coming down still rang in her ears and dust and powdered concrete still rained down from above.

"Shut yer trap," Nick said, in the middle of hacking the dust from his lungs. "We're fine. Check the grate."

All three men aimed their flashlights toward the spot where the grate once was to see that not only had the bars yielded, but so had a large chunk of the surrounding wall, making an easy access for them all. Nick briefly chuckled his approval. Everything was going right for him tonight, Leena figured he was thinking. Little did he know what she had planned for him.

~ Chapter 8 ~

After a brief respite, the rain again started to fall. Slowly at first, little more than a trickle, but it didn't take long to build from there, reaching a crescendo which was by now very familiar to the people of Metro. Detective Bob Sloan, standing in a tapered street a few blocks from the Metro docks, craned his head upward, allowing the water to drench his face. In a city this dirty, he felt that the water from the heavens above was somehow cleansing, and not just physically. Sloan often thought his soul needed cleansing. Living almost all your life in a city such as Metro, where crime ruled, where indecency reigned and working for years amongst a sea of corruption could do that to a person.

Sloan wiped the excess water from his face and focused on the job at hand. He adjusted the cap on his head and crouched down beside his partner Rosa Perez, who was examining another body, this one discovered in a dumpster.

"Another one, Bob. Another victim. Heart removed, same as the others," she said.

"Any I.D. on him?"

"Yeah," she replied, standing, then motioned to a nearby C.S.I officer, who made his way over to them.

The officer held an umbrella over Perez's head while handing her a small evidence bag. "He was carrying his wallet, no money or cards appear to have been taken. His name was Robert Oscar. Forty five years old. We're checking his background now, but I doubt there'll be anything to find."

Sloan rubbed at his eyes. So much misery and death and it seemed as though it was never-ending. He was tough, always had been, which was why he'd made it so far and for so long in a city like Metro. Nevertheless, it was starting to gnaw at his soul, bit by bit, case by case. He wondered if he should take a vacation, maybe get away from it all for a while. Such thoughts had been rare over the years, despite his wife's regular pleas. But now, those feelings had come much more often, and that surprised him. He'd long prided himself on his strength. Strength of character, strength of justice and courage. And loyalty. He somehow felt responsible to his partner, to his commissioner, to the police force, to the city as a whole. He remembered better times in Metro, and somehow felt like those times could come again. But if he gave up, what chance was there then? It was a lot to put on one man's shoulders, but Sloan had done this his entire career, and despite his weariness, he knew he had to go on. Too much was at stake.

"Bag him and send him over to Howard," Sloan said. "I want every last detail of the body examined and re-examined. His clothing, his possessions, everything. There has to be something that links him to the others, something that can give us a lead on this serial killer. We have that piece of rag from the last victim. Tell Howard to cross-reference that with anything found on Oscar."

"Right," Perez said, and retreated quickly alongside the C.S.I. officer.

Sloan took a few steps back, allowing the relevant officials to remove the body and send it on its way to the morgue. His thoughts briefly turned to the subject of Aztekoth, to the night when the creature's appearance at the City Gallery had caused such a commotion. The escalation in the serial killer case had taken him and Perez away from that. He cursed himself for allowing this to happen. He had wanted to further question both Paul Sanderson and Robert Latham on what had actually happened, but hadn't been able to do either. Yet. He promised himself that he'd get back on top of things. The police force was seriously undermanned, yes, but even so, it had to be done.

He allowed himself a few more moments of thought before turning and marching through the sodden night toward his car. He was going to get some answers, and soon.

* * * * * *

The Wraith awoke with a thumping headache. Worse still, he found himself strung up, chained to the wall in an unknown location. He tried to move, but all he achieved was sending sharp slivers of pain throughout his body. His bindings clanked in stubborn refusal. He wasn't going anywhere.

Where am I? How did I get here?

The Wraith tried remembering what had occurred. Then it all came back to him. He'd been trailing the skeletons through the city, finally reaching an abandoned warehouse and an obvious trap. He'd thought himself clever in avoiding it, and yet here he was. He cursed his own foolishness and his underestimating the enemy. Like an amateur, he allowed himself to be lured and captured with amazing ease. Anger rose within him, and he again attempted escape, hoping for at least some sign of movement from the chains, but there was almost no give.

He forced himself to calm down, to relax as best he could. With more clarity of thought, the Dread Avenger examined his surrounds. It was dark, and he had no chance of switching on his night-vision lenses, but he could tell he was in a small room with cobblestone brick walls. And...

A door suddenly snapped open and a blinding light shone in his face. He turned away, struggling to adjust his vision to the new lighting conditions. Momentarily blinded, the clunking footfalls of several individuals soon filled the room.

Hard floor too.

His eyes slowly focused. Several skeletal warriors advanced toward him, brandishing spears and shields.

The three skeletons stopped just short of him and stood there side-by-side. The entire room was cobblestoned. It was small, akin to a castle's dungeon, complete with the chain fastenings to which he found himself imprisoned while the door appeared to be constructed of an ancient, and thick, metal of some kind.

The Wraith's eyes narrowed as the skeletons stood there, silent and still, before him. The hairs on the back of his neck stood on edge.

What are they here for? What are they waiting for?

The eerie atmosphere was not dispelled by the sudden appearance of their leader, the monstrous Aztekoth, whose feet hovered mere inches from the ground. Not with any kind of grace, however. It appeared to move through the air with great ease, but there was an unnaturalness to it. The Wraith couldn't help but tremor within. The creature's presence...

The skeletons parted, allowing their leader to move toward him.

"Infidel," the creature said. "What purpose have you here?"

The Wraith remained silent, eying the creature carefully through narrow slits. Despite how experienced and hardened as he was, Aztekoth was a hideous sight. The skeletal hands protruding from the filthy, torn rags that made up the creature's entire outfit were foreboding enough, but the sight of the shrunken skull hanging around Aztekoth's neck, as well as a string of large, razor-sharp canine-like teeth sent shivers down his spine. But it was the creature's stench, which smelled musty, decrepit, fetid, almost like—*rotting flesh?*—turned The Wraith's stomach.

"You refuse to answer? Curious," Aztekoth said as it loomed even closer to The Wraith's face. "You cannot possibly comprehend what you are dealing with."

The Wraith decided to again remain silent, waiting for an indication of the creature's intent or purpose.

"I could destroy you with a simple touch, Wraith. Such is the power of my curse."

He knows my name. "Curse?" The Wraith finally said, his interest piqued.

Aztekoth took a step back, faced the skeletons and mockingly huffed. "Yes, curse. My followers and I were cursed for worshiping the great Huitzilopochtli with 'too much zeal.' The fools, the arrant fools! Our great god was our salvation against the invading hordes. My people should have realized, should have listened."

So, he's human after all. The Wraith wanted to know more, much more. "Tell me about this curse."

Aztekoth faced him again. "Perhaps I should ask more questions of you? Who are you, Wraith? What is your purpose? Are you so foolish as to engage me so openly? Perhaps I should just annihilate you now..."

The creature drew even closer. The stench was now overwhelming and a sharp bubble of bile stung the back of The Wraith's throat.

Aztekoth paused then and appeared to look the Dread Avenger over carefully, turning his head slightly from side-to-side, despite The Wraith not being able to see into the murky darkness of the creature's hood, save for his penetrating, glowing red eyes.

"No, I will not kill you. Yet," he said. "You are no threat to me, but you...interest me, Wraith. You are unique. That much, at least, we have in common. We will meet again. Soon. Perhaps then you will be more willing to talk."

Aztekoth turned and moved for the door. He exited without a further word. The skeletal warriors re-grouped, glared at The Wraith, then proceeded to follow their leader.

The door slammed shut and The Wraith was alone again.

What was the point of that? The Wraith thought. *A fishing expedition, naturally, but why keep me here? What is this thing up to? I have to learn more, why is he here, how is he able to do these horrendous things? And figure out a way to escape. It won't be easy...*

He tried to loosen himself from his bonds once more, but again they refused to yield. There had to be another way. It would take time to ascertain a plan of escape. It looked as though, for now, he had that time. He set himself to that very task and began to think things through.

* * * * * *

The group climbed up onto the platform of the long abandoned Stanton Station. Leena settled herself there, and scanned her surroundings. Dilapidated as it was, it was still recognizable as what it was once meant to be, a subway station for the then ever-expanding city. Now, of course, it was run-down, filthy, its buildings ramshackle and broken. The platforms themselves, however, seemed as sturdy as ever. No evidence of concrete cancer that Leena could discern.

A light strobed on from above. Dave poked his head from the door of what appeared to be the station master's office.

"I found the light switch."

"It must be around here somewhere," Nick said impatiently. "Check for gratings in the floor."

Everyone scuttled around, including Eddie, though he was meant to be watching Leena closely. He had no idea that she was not yet ready to pounce. She was biding her time, waiting for the right moment.

Where's Paul? she thought.

She was sure she would have felt his presence by now, or he would have somehow made himself known to her. But up 'til now, nothing. She was not worried, however. She knew the love of her life too well for that. He had promised to be there. And he had never broken such a promise to her.

So, for now, she waited. And watched.

~ Chapter 9 ~

After some minutes searching, Dave shouted, "Over here. I think I found it."

The others rushed over, including Leena, to where Dave was crouched down, peering into a small grate on the platform floor.

"Lemme see," Nick said, pushing Dave aside. He dropped to the ground, flashed his light down into the hole. "Yes, yes, I see it. There it is!"

Leena stood over them and looked down through the metal grate. It was hard to make out from the angle and distance, but there appeared to be a wooden crate down there.

"Get the hammers," Nick said. "We need to break this open."

Dave went and pulled two small sledge hammers from his backpack.

"All right, let's go," Nick told him.

Each took a hammer and let loose, while Eddie continued to watch over Leena. Nick and Dave sweated and puffed as they worked diligently. With each blast of their hammers, dust and chunks of concrete flew. Eddie began coughing with increasing regularity. Leena wondered how much longer he could stand it before cracking.

"C'mon, put yer back into it," Nick growled. He was by now sweating profusely, and was clearly frustrated at their distinct lack of progress.

Dave wheezed heavily from the dust cloud now enveloping the two of them, which only impeded their progress even more. Leena wondered whether he was suffering from a mild form of asthma.

The minutes dragged on, with Nick insisting they continue slogging away. Eddie was forced back, his coughing having become violent, as he attempted to avoid as much of the billowing dust as possible. He was, by now, no longer watching Leena, interested only in his own well-being.

Good, she thought.

Something moved...there! To the side. Finally. The sign she had been waiting for. She carefully vacated the scene, using the dust cloud as a shield.

* * * * * *

After much effort, the two men were finally making some significant progress. Large chunks of concrete were now being spewed forth with each blow, and they were slowly, but surely, edging down further. Several more minutes later, they broke down into the drain itself.

"The light, quickly," Nick said.

Dave climbed back up and scrambled for his flashlight. In moments, he was standing over the large hole, shining the light downward on Nick and their prize.

"The plates are mine. Finally," Nick shrieked.

He clutched the box and fidgeted with the lock. He couldn't get a good handle on it given the angle. "Help me get this up outta here."

Nick heaved the box up above his head and handed it to Dave, who plunked it down beside the hole on the platform floor. Nick climbed out of the drain and joined Dave, both eying the box intently.

Nick grabbed his sledge hammer and smashed the lock open with relative ease. He opened the box, his eyes widening. "It's here."

He pulled a cloth-wrapped object from the box, held it gently as if it were a newborn babe before carefully unwrapping it. Beneath the cloth were several plates for the printing of five dollar notes, all in perfect condition, as though new.

Before he could say anything, there was a thud behind them. It was then he realized there was no sign of the girl. He couldn't even see Eddie anymore. *Has he bailed on us?* He quickly re-wrapped the plates.

Both Nick and Dave turned toward the direction of the noise. Dave gasped. Nick was stunned into silence. There, standing before them, his cape wrapped around him like a vampiric creature at rest, was The Wraith Dread Avenger of the Underworld.

"Hand those plates over," The Wraith boomed. "They are not for the likes of you."

Eddie suddenly appeared from nowhere, obviously panicking. Screaming, he leaped from the platform and landed in a heap on the gravel. He was up as quickly as possible, and made a run for it along the aged railway tracks, soon vanishing into the darkness.

Nick and Dave remained rooted to the spot, not daring to move, not knowing what to do next.

Nick soon regained his courage. "Come take it from us then," he snarled.

The Wraith walked forward, his cape still wrapped around him. Dave held his nerve for a moment, but as The Wraith loomed closer, he too panicked and attempted escape. As he turned to flee, a powerful hand grabbed his shoulder and whirled him back around. The Wraith lashed out with a mighty right to the jaw, sending Dave sprawling into unconsciousness.

Nick growled, his anger fueled. He had come so close—*so close*—but to only have it all snatched from him now? No, he wouldn't give up. Not yet. He grabbed the wrapped-up plates, and leaped from the platform down onto the tracks, making a more dignified landing than Eddie had. With the plates still securely in his grasp, he sprinted for the direction of the rope, leading up into the sewer tunnel from where they came.

That fool, he thought. *He's run off in the wrong direction. There's no escape that way.*

The light from the train station behind him began to dim as he continued his headlong flight into the darkness. He hadn't been able to bring along his light, but he then realized what a blessing that had been. With no light, the better he could merge into the blackness and make his escape.

The rope couldn't be that much further, could it?

In mid-stride, something entangled his ankles, causing him to topple forward and slam face first into the gravel. He couldn't stop himself from grunting in pain; his hands still protected his valuable cargo. He rolled over onto his back. A trickle or two of blood ran down his face. It was dark. Not totally black, the light from the platform was still vaguely visible in the distance, but enough to make visibility next to impossible. His mind was racing. What had snagged his feet? He reached down to try and feel, to pull himself free. Then he heard it—footsteps on gravel. Softly at first, then louder, as though...coming closer. He strained to see in the darkness. The faint, distant light was still there, and yet, he could make out nothing else. What was going on? The noise became louder and louder with each passing second. Nick began to panic, clutching at the cord tightly wound around his ankles.

Why won't it come free?

"You cannot escape me," a deep, booming voice emerged from nowhere and everywhere at the same time.

Nick, frantic, tried again to free his feet, but the cord was too tight and he couldn't get his fingers between it and his ankles. His breathing increased and sweat streamed down his face. He whined with fear.

"Now is your time of punishment," The Wraith said, appearing in front of him, pointing at him.

Nick could only stammer in reply.

Before he could even blink, The Wraith yanked him up off the ground.

"Of judgment!"

* * * * * *

Eddie ran as fast as his weak legs would carry him. He couldn't see, as he ran toward the darkest area he could find, but he didn't care. He just wanted to get away, to hide. He never wanted to be there in the first place, and coming face-to-face with The Wraith had never been on his agenda either. This whole thing was wrong. *Wrong.* But there had been no way out of it. He was too weak to deny Nick, and he had nowhere else to go. In a sick twist of fate, Nick was all he had, all the family he had ever known. In his current situation, however, he regretted ever knowing him, and cursed his own helplessness, his own stupidity. Still, he wasn't being followed, he could still get away. He could start again, start a new life.

Sure, why not? He thought. If he could just get out of this hell-hole, there would be no stopping him. Nothing at all.

An incredibly bright light shot out from nowhere, blinding him. *Who could this be? Oh no, not the—*

A stranger appeared. No one he knew and definitely not The Wraith. Eddie breathed a little easier, relieved.

"What are you doing here?" the stranger asked in a thick, Irish accent.

"N—nothing," was all Eddie could reply.

"Well, here. Let me help you to safety," the stranger said. He looked friendly enough, dressed something like an...English gentleman? With thick, red sideburns and a broad smile on his face. The stranger moved over to Eddie's side.

Eddie smiled, felt himself fortunate. He wanted to thank the stranger, thank him for his kindness. He—

He found himself lying in a heap on the ground. Everything had happened in such a blur that Eddie was momentarily confused. Then he felt the pain in his jaw.

"Come on, the safety of a cell awaits you," the stranger said.

Eddie caught on to what was going on. This person was an agent of The Wraith.

He screamed.

* * * * * *

It was extremely late, but Sloan didn't care. He plopped himself down at his desk, frustrated. He and his partner had just returned from the morgue where Howard Boynce, the city's chief medical examiner, had nothing much to report. The cloth found with the body of Richard Stanley matched some threads found on the body of the most recent victim, Robert Oscar. The material was very old, and not from this country, but apart from that, Howard had been unable to tell them more. Sloan rubbed at his temples. It had been a long night, and all he really wanted to do was curl up in bed and sleep forever. He couldn't even remember the last time he'd gotten a good night's rest. He sometimes felt he may never be able to again.

"Bob, don't go there," Perez said.

Sloan barely registered Perez's presence. He rubbed at his temples some more, then tried rubbing his eyes to rid himself of the cobwebs. Finally, he said, "Perez, I'm tired. I'm tired of this whole thing!"

"It's this case, I know..."

"It's not just this case," Sloan said wearily. "It's everything. It's this whole city. If it was only going down the toilet, that would be one thing, but we have serial killers running amok and creatures from the stuff of nightmares..."

Sloan knew things were different now. He'd felt exhaustion coming on before, many a time in fact. But nothing like this. It was an indescribable feeling. He just knew something was wrong. Really wrong. Yet whether it was unique to just himself or it was due to the current horrific situation being experienced throughout the city—or both—he had no idea.

Perez bent over him, concern written all over her face. "Bob, what's wrong? I mean, what's really wrong? No case has ever troubled you like this before, at least not since the Reeve case. We've tackled worse than this. You can tell me."

That was just it: he didn't *know* what was wrong. Whatever it was gnawing at his soul, it wasn't anything he could put into words. And that troubled him, more than he cared to admit. As he always did, however, he shrugged it off. He prided himself on his strength, his character, and he wasn't about to allow some touchy-feely stuff to break him down now.

"It's nothing, Perez. Really."

He stood, as though to stop her from asking any more questions on the subject, and began pacing behind his desk. Perez got the message and remained silent.

After a few moments, Sloan said, "Well, we at least have confirmation that we're dealing with the same killer or killers, not that we doubted that. It gives us something, though I'd hoped Howard would have been able to give us more."

"The cloth was really old, ancient, in fact. Howard emphasized that point," Perez added. "He couldn't pinpoint a date, but he did say it was of foreign origin."

"Which tells us very little in the end," Sloan said. "It's something, I know, but I'd hoped for more." He started pacing again.

"These are just the preliminary results, Bob. Howard will come back to us with something more solid."

"I hope so. Because without enough evidence, this killer will go on killing. This is not over yet. Not by a long shot."

* * * * * *

Max sat pensively behind the wheel of the classic Daimler he mostly drove as the Sanderson chauffeur. He would often escort either Paul or Leena for social and business occasions. Other times, always at night, he would guide the Dread Avenger of the Underworld, often with Leena in tow, through his war on crime in Metro. Now he sat alone, waiting.

In the blink of an eye, The Wraith appeared in the rear passenger seat, startling him.

"Jeez, you've mastered the Chief's act," Max blurted.

Leena removed the cowl from her head, tousled the sweat from her hair. "Thanks. I've worked hard enough at it. And this suit of yours disguises my shape perfectly. Thanks for bringing it along." She removed the voice imitator from the neckline of her suit, and said in her own voice, "We have the missing plates and the police will be mopping up those thugs shortly. I'm glad I caught your signal, though I was surprised to see you there and not Paul."

"The Chief hasn't been in contact since he went out on patrol," Max revealed. "I'm not one to worry, but...this feels different somehow. Something's going on in this city, something I can't put my finger on."

"What with Aztekoth and what we've seen of him, I'm not surprised."

"It's not Aztekoth, I know that much," Max said. "Don't ask me how or why. I just know this is something different, something more." A brief pause. "There's a blackness falling over this city. I can't describe it any better than that."

There was a brief moment of silence, as though neither knew what to say. Max thought momentarily about what he'd just said. How could he really know this feeling he was currently experiencing wasn't just caused by Aztekoth, by the events of a few days ago? In truth, it wasn't something he could justify, or even put into proper words. He just knew deep down that despite the horrific events at the City Gallery something else was amiss in Metro. Something potentially worse. And with the Chief missing in action till now, that worried him.

While these concerns ruminated in his mind, Leena spoke up. "Do you have a make on his location?"

"No, he hasn't switched his locator beacon on. Another reason to worry."

"Well, let's drive through the city and hope we hear something from him soon. I'll get changed in the meantime." She pulled down the center console and began placing bits and pieces from her specially designed Wraith suit into the slot.

Max felt like this was going to be a long night. He turned the key over and directed the car out of the side alley and into the busy city traffic.

~ Chapter 10 ~

The Wraith continued to struggle against his bonds. It was now no longer a question of escape; that was not possible. His shackles were somewhat rusted, but thus far, immovable. But if he could just reach his locator beacon in his gauntlet, switch it on...

Movement. The shackles over his right wrist started to come loose. Only very slightly, but enough to fill The Wraith with the renewed hope of escape.

Perhaps they're more rusted than I thought.

He battled on, huffing with exertion. His muscles strained, his shoulder ached, but he pressed on, pulling with as much might as he could muster with so little leverage. Gradually, his toil began to bear fruit, as the large bolt holding the shackle in place began to loosen and gave him more room to move. With one last heave, he jerked his right arm upward, freeing it, though his wrist was still shackled.

Finally. Now to activate the beacon.

Which he did so with relative ease. His belt had been removed, so he was at the disadvantage of not being able to use the equipment contained within it, but he had a free arm, which was enough to work at liberating his left arm, and once that was done, his legs. It was tough going; the remaining shackles were held tightly in place and took some work before they even started to loosen, let alone come free. In time, however, The Wraith stood in his dungeon; bent over, heaving with exhaustion, his arms and legs still burdened with shackles around the wrists and ankles. But he was free.

Now, how do I get out of this cell? It's going to be a problem without my belt.

As soon as he thought this, a noise came from outside the cell door.

A guard?

The Dread Avenger stole a peek through the small window in the door. A burly Indian patrolled the corridor, outfitted as the skeletons had been.

An Aztec?

There was no time for further delay. The Wraith moved over to one side, and whispered. The guard outside grunted and peered into the cell. The door swung open and the guard made a noise of apparent shock. Then The Wraith pounced from his vantage point behind the door, leaping onto the Indian, attacking with everything he had. Two roundhouse punches to the face, and the battle was over.

With the Indian lying unconscious on the cobblestoned floor, The Wraith searched him for the key to his shackles. Sure enough, he found them, used them and shook the shackles and chains loose from his wrists and ankles.

Moving stealthily over to the door, he inspected the corridor for any sign of life. There was none. Carefully, he inched out into the corridor and, briefly considering the direction he would take, turned right. He didn't know why, it just *felt* right.

The corridor was lined with wooden torches, providing enough illumination to move by. The air was thick, musty, aged. Dust and cobwebs littered the walls at their upper levels, and dirt lined the floor, causing his heavy boots to scrape against the cobblestoned flooring with each step. There was nowhere to hide if anyone were to come toward him; no side doors or access ways—nothing.

He continued his way through the lengthy corridor.

Is there even an end? He had no idea.

There was no alternative but to continue on. He felt like an experimental rat being led through a maze, and even though he hadn't been walking all that long, it still seemed like it.

Then he heard it.

What is that? Sounds like some kind of...ceremony?

He carefully rounded a corner and found himself faced with two doors, one open, the other closed. The noise, now much louder and fevered, came from the open door. The Wraith entered it. Through the arched doorway, a narrower corridor led him to an alcove that ended in a balcony overlooking a great hall. Crouched down in the dust, he cautiously looked over the parapet, down to the hall and toward the building cacophony below him.

The hall was extremely large and intricately detailed, with arched wood beam ceilings, stone walls and sagging wooden floors. The walls were lined with blazing torches and Aztec shields, statues and jewelry, ornaments featuring snakes and dragons and a series of turquoise masks. Pews, like those contained within any western church, filled the entire center portion of the hall. Within the pews were seated a mixture of Aztec Indian and skeletal warriors, both garbed as those he'd seen earlier, all facing a large, raised platform. He craned his neck for a better look, hoping he wouldn't be discovered in doing so.

On the platform—more or less a stage which at its rear featured a giant mosaic of the Aztec war god Huitzilopochtli —stood the creature Aztekoth, holding something aloft, something bloody. What, The Wraith couldn't tell. But he feared the worst.

"This heart will revive another of our fallen," Aztekoth cried. "One more of our damned brethren will be reborn through the sacrifice of this city's sinners. Defilers of the sacred stone!"

It was a human heart that the monster was holding. The Wraith's stomach twisted. He cursed the fact he'd been too late to save whomever it once belonged to. He now realized that Aztekoth and his band of Aztecs were behind the recent wave of serial killings in Metro City. It wasn't some lone psychopath, some modern day Jack the Ripper, nor some group trading in stolen organs. No, it was something far more sinister. Far more deadly.

The Wraith watched in horror as Aztekoth turned and carried the bloodied organ over to what appeared to be a long wooden crate.

Or a coffin? he thought.

It was hard for him to see past the Aztekoth's imposing figure, but the creature appeared to bend over the crate.

"Rise now, my brother. Claim the life that was wrongfully taken from you. Rise and reclaim the empire that spurned you, but that we will rebuild, here. Rise!"

Aztekoth turned to face his followers, and it was then that The Wraith saw what had transpired. A skeleton now stood before the creature, but it was its chest which both amazed and chilled him to the core. The bloodied heart, obviously just procured from its victim, was now securely in place within the ribcage of the walking skeleton. The Wraith blinked in horror.

The warrior slowly trudged over to the far end of the platform, where some Indians, outfitted as all the others with traditional robes, shield and a spear, fitted the newcomer with likewise. It then joined the dozens of other living skeletons seated in the front row of the hall, the chanting having built to a fever pitch during this ceremony.

The Wraith turned, ducked back down under the railing and sat leaning up against it. His mind raced as he came to grips with the realities of the situation. Aztekoth, by some amazing act of wizardry, was bringing to life its dead followers of a bygone era, using the hearts of the murdered innocents of the city as replacement organs.

It needs the Cortes Stone in some way as well, he thought. *But how? And why?*

Thoughts of his current predicament returned to him. How could he get out of there and alert the authorities? He had no idea of the location of this foul place, so decided it best to attempt to discover that as soon as possible. Once he'd done that, then he would determine his next course of action. He decided to take one last look at the goings on below before moving on.

Carefully peering over once more, The Wraith came face-to-face with a human skull. Momentarily stunned, The Wraith quickly moved into action, grabbing the skeletal warrior by the head and sent him back down into the hall.

Shouts and murmurs rose from below.

Great, he thought. *I've been spotted.*

"Get him!" Aztekoth shouted. "Do not let him escape!"

Several skeletal warriors had already been climbing up toward the balcony and now the remaining warriors, both alive and undead, were mobilizing.

The Wraith had to move fast. His belt missing, there was no other option: he had to backtrack and attempt to escape that way. Exiting via the arched doorway, the sounds of fast-approaching footfalls greeted him. The Wraith turned in the opposite direction, sprinting down the dank, dim corridor, hoping upon hope to find a swift exit from this place.

This particular corridor twisted and turned, but there were no other branches, no doors, which encouraged the Dread Avenger. Perhaps this was indeed the way out. He could still hear the noise of the band pursuing him. As he swiftly rounded the next bend, he ran straight into Max and Leena.

"Darling," Leena started, breathless.

"No time," The Wraith said. "We have to get out of here. Now!"

Without a further word, the trio spun on their heels and ran.

"The exit is down this way," Max said, leading the way.

Rounding another sharp bend, a large, intricate wooden door loomed in the center, with two other, smaller doors on either side.

"The center door, that's the exit," Max said.

Upon reaching it, Max yanked at the handle, pulling it open with a slight squeaking of hinges.

Aztekoth stood before them.

* * * * * *

Smoke wafted up to the ceiling of the well-adorned meeting room within the Latham Industries building. Cigar in hand, Robert Latham sat at the head of the long, cylindrical-shaped mahogany table. To his right sat his right-hand man, Charlie Grieco. Beside Grieco, and to Latham's left, were other highly-placed capos within his organization, most of which were smoking cigarettes or cigars.

"So, you're all telling me that profits are up and overheads are down?" Latham said.

"Yes, sir. Profits have never been higher, both with our legitimate concerns and our other, varied enterprises," Grieco replied.

"Drug imports have risen by over forty percent, fueled by demand," said a particularly corpulent individual. "The increased yield in countries such as Afghanistan have greatly contributed to this." He chuckled. "Why, the Taliban is still in the game because of us."

"Increased demand, you say? We've managed to find buyers for all our product?" Latham enquired of his overweight staff member.

"Oh, indeed. There's never been a lack of buyers in Metro for high quality Heroin, and our increased distribution network since the disbursement of the Tzi group has helped facilitate this."

"Splendid," Latham said, taking a nice, long puff on his stogie. "Weapons sales have also increased, I take it?"

A slimmer and older man replied. "By over sixty percent, mostly to Afghanistan and certain African countries. The various civil wars throughout those regions have helped us enormously."

Latham stood, his mood boosted by the positive news. He smiled. "Wonderful; just the kind of news that makes my day. We've consolidated and grown our business here in

Metro and managed to increase profits throughout our worldwide endeavors. I expect further such increases during the next quarter." He sidled over to stand behind his deputy Grieco. "Now, Charlie" —he took another, shorter puff— "tell me your good news."

Grieco looked up at Latham with penetrating eyes. "Good news?"

"Yes, of your discovery of the creature Aztekoth. Of how you discovered his lair and took care of him for me."

Grieco stuttered briefly. "But, I—"

Latham backhanded him, landing a powerful blow to the side of Grieco's head. Grieco went flying from his seat and onto the plush maroon carpet. He recovered quickly, though, sat up facing Latham, his eyes hot with rage. The deputy said nothing, however.

Latham's staff began to murmur at the display of rage.

"The reality of the situation is that nothing has been done and the creature has been allowed to roam my city unperturbed, ultimately resulting in its attack on me in my own home," Latham outlined. "I, however, took charge and dealt with the monster—personally. We can now rest easy, for the creature is dead." He reached down and helped Grieco to his feet. A small amount of blood trickled from the deputy's ear due to the power of Latham's savage blow. "Now, perhaps we can ensure the rest of this city's program can proceed without further disruption?"

Grieco merely nodded and sat back down in his chair.

"Good. Now, what's been done regarding the replacement for Bartholomew Gregory?" Latham asked him.

"We have several superbly qualified candidates on the short list," Grieco said. "We're beginning to narrow them down now."

"Excellent, though we need to hurry. I want a new man in place by the time of the street parade. This Aztekoth has already cost me time and money, neither of which I care to lose under any circumstances. The creature is dead. Nothing need stand in our way of presenting a fitting parade for the two hundredth anniversary of my city." Latham walked past Grieco to alongside his other staff members, who watched on eagerly, fear and apprehension clearly written on their faces. Latham loved this, loved intimidating everyone around him. For it was fear, as much as anything else, which consolidated his power in Metro, and he exercised it where and when he could. "I fully intend to proceed with plans for the Cortes Stone to be the centerpiece of the entire parade. The people will know I, and I alone, am responsible for this parade, and the success of it, and they will also know by the end of it who truly runs this city."

Latham continued walking slowly, around the far end of the table and back toward his own seat. When he sat down, he took another puff on his Cuban.

"But, Mr. Latham," Grieco began. "Isn't that a little dangerous? After what we've seen the stone capable of, and what with Aztekoth..."

"Aztekoth is dead!" Latham snapped. "Do you dare go against my word? After your own recent failure in carrying out my instructions, I would choose your next words very carefully."

Grieco appeared somewhat befuddled, but continued as before. "No, I just think we should continue to err on the side of caution with things we do not yet understand."

Latham calmed somewhat. "Charlie, Charlie, relax. I have cleaned up your mess. I understand your initial reticence, but you needn't worry. The matter has been dealt with and is as good as forgotten." He stood, remained upright, facing his troops. "We will move forward as planned. Meeting adjourned."

Everyone stood and shuffled out of the room. Grieco was about to do likewise, but was stopped by Latham, who had remained rooted to the spot.

"Charlie...don't ever go against an order during a meeting again. If you have concerns, bring them to my office and we can discuss them personally, man to man," Latham said. "The Cortes Stone is my key to legitimate power in this city. I own it already. Not even The Wraith can take that from me, try as he might. But I want more. Much more." He placed his cigar in his mouth and smiled, holding the door of the meeting room open for Grieco without yet letting him exit. "I want it all, you hear me? And this parade is merely the beginning of my plans. And nothing or no one is going to stand in my way, least of all you."

Grieco registered understanding on his face, but said nothing. Latham bowed ever so slightly, indicating the door, and Grieco exited quickly. Latham stood there, watching his deputy slinking off with his tail between his legs.

Good, he thought, smiling again. *It all starts here.*

~ Chapter 11 ~

Aztekoth advanced toward the trio, looming like some real-life Grim Reaper. There was a stark chill in the air.

"You seek to escape? Such foolishness," the creature moaned. "There is no escape for the likes of you."

Aztekoth stood in the rounded, open doorway.

Thinking quickly, The Wraith cried out, "Scatter."

Max and Leena reacted with immediacy, each choosing one of the open doorways on either side of the exit. Now, The Wraith faced Aztekoth alone.

"Those corridors lead nowhere but into the heart of our empire's new capital," Aztekoth said. "There is no escape there."

The Wraith stood resolutely in place, Aztekoth's monstrous form not fazing him. Without his belt, his options were limited, but he had to allow time for Max and

Leena to somehow escape. Despite all the odds, he could still take care of himself. He had to make his stand here.

"I grow weary of you, Wraith," Aztekoth said. "Perhaps it is time to rid myself of a gnat such as you."

The creature extended a bony arm, intending to end things there and then. The Wraith knew all too well the power the monster possessed. Aztekoth extended another arm, as if to grab his jaw or throat. Then he remembered back to that evening at the city gallery. The creature had grabbed that security guard by the arm—his bare arm.

It requires contact with the skin, The Wraith realized, and breathed a small sigh of relief while at the same time dodging the creature's outstretched arms.

The Wraith took a step back, out of the immediate range of Aztekoth's fingers. "Why do you want the stone?"

"The stone is our salvation," Aztekoth revealed. "The rebirth of our race—our empire—is dependent on it. It is sacred, not to be looked upon by those who disbelieve, by those not one of us."

Aztekoth pushed forward, appearing to glide along the dusty ground as though skating along an iced-over lake in Metro's Hyde Park. It made a grab for The Wraith, who attempted to fight back with powerful punches to the creature's midsection. It was though he were punching a brick wall. Strangely enough, The Wraith could tell it wasn't as bony of body as it was in its arms, and yet, there was some flesh there, though the creature acted as though nothing had happened, as though it were completely invulnerable. The Wraith wondered what had brought the creature to such a fate, and wondered what he could do to stop such a powerful adversary. The struggle continued. Aztekoth had its immense size as an advantage, and it was incredibly strong. It reached forward, again trying to apply its deathly touch to The

Wraith's face, but the Dread Avenger countered by grabbing both its arms, and holding them at bay with all his might.

"Accept death as your rightful destiny," Aztekoth groaned. "Become a part of the greatest empire this world has ever known, and will know again."

It intends to kill me and use my heart to revive another of its tribe, The Wraith thought. *That's the purpose of all these slayings...it intends to revive the entire Aztec race!*

"You intend your new empire to be positioned here, in the US?"

"This is the most powerful nation in the world, and soon it will truly be so."

"It is you who are the fool, Aztekoth," The Wraith said, still struggling to hold the creature off. "Even if you were to take over the entire city, the government would send the army against you. You haven't a chance against such odds."

"Never underestimate me," Aztekoth boomed, wrenching its arms free and connecting with a backhand to The Wraith's jaw, sending him flying backward through the air.

The Wraith landed in a heap in the dirt, and rubbed his jaw ruefully. Not only did it feel as though it had been broken, but there was the sensation of having been burned, badly, on the right side of his face. He guessed that, for some reason, a short amount of exposure to Aztekoth's touch was not lethal, at least not for him, but extremely painful, resulting in burns of considerable strength.

Aztekoth moved toward the prone Dread Avenger. "We have influence within the corridors of power, in this city, in this state, within the White House itself. Everything has been planned, nothing can stop us from being whole again and fulfilling our destiny!"

The Wraith, attempting surprise, leaped to his feet, thinking to perhaps catch the creature off-guard and sidestep past it. But Aztekoth was too quick, its size belying its speed and strength. It grabbed The Wraith by his shoulders, its deathly touch actually beginning to burn through the armor of his costume. The heat was incredible, and the Dread Avenger could not help but groan in pain. It was now clear that while the creature's touch was not immediately deadly on anything but skin, with prolonged exposure, even his armor would prove ineffectual.

"Now you begin to feel the fiery touch of Aztekoth. Sinners will burn for all eternity. You will be reborn as a warrior of a most blessed race, a leader of men within my empire."

The pain was becoming unbearable. The Wraith feared he would soon black out, such was the intensity of the searing pain throughout his shoulders. It was as though he were standing in the middle of a blazing inferno, such was the feeling of intense burning, but it was somehow also more than that. The shooting pain reached right down to his soul in a way that was almost impossible to describe, but was nevertheless gut-wrenching to endure. The Wraith struggled to break free with what little strength remained to him, but Aztekoth held him firmly, his grip like iron. Could this be the end? Could it end like this, with his city at the mercy of such a creature from Hell?

No, not like this, not while Leena and Max have yet to escape. Leena...

Then all went black.

* * * * * *

The smell alone was enough to make oneself sick, but Leena had already experienced enough that night to last a lifetime. She found herself again crawling through the fetid sewers of Metro City, this time in the process escaping the clutches of the heinous creature known as Aztekoth. She had instantly realized what Paul had meant, and adhered to his instructions. Working with the Dread Avenger as closely as she had, she knew his word was the rule. She worried, though. How could she not? Despite his incredible abilities, his great strength and skill, she worried he would prove no match for such as Aztekoth. She chided herself for such thoughts, but they re-surfaced soon enough. She had seen at least some of what Aztekoth was capable of, knew well some of the supernatural power it possessed. And her beloved was now all alone up against such a monstrosity. She battled the urge to turn back, to help him in some way, though she knew not how.

She stopped herself, however. She knew where one might escape successfully, two might not. Without nothing but his physical strength and his brains, Leena knew deep down Paul would be no match for Aztekoth, that escape to fight another day would be his only option. She found some inner strength there and then, and continued inching her way along the narrowest of sewers, the entry to which she had located at the farthest end of the corridor she had entered; through the filthy, putrid liquid and feculant matter toward ultimate safety. She would see her beloved again. He would probably be already home once she arrived. Such thoughts gave Leena added strength, and she continued as quickly as her surrounds allowed her to.

* * * * * *

Max wondered exactly where he was. It was dark, darker than anything he'd ever experienced. He had run, as the Chief had bidden him, into the doorway nearest him, and kept running as far as the tunnel allowed. But he had soon reached a dead end, and had then scrambled around in the darkness for any sign of further advancement. The tunnel had clearly shrunken the further he had run, for he could easily feel either side, even the ceiling of it, without too much lateral movement. He was fully equipped, naturally, but feared the use of his penlight would give away his location to any possible pursuers (though he heard none), and he knew how important the Chief thought his and Leena's escape was.

He tried to remain as silent as possible within the inky void, but feared his breathlessness might give himself away. He had stood still, leaned against the wall, and composed himself as best he could, controlling his breathing, normalizing his nerves. He had strained to hear anything at all, but all was silent. He had obviously run further than he thought, for he could not hear anything from the battle scene he had just fled.

Fled.

The word bit hard within Max's psyche. He was not a coward. Far from it. If asked, he would have faced Aztekoth right there and then, to the death if need be. But deep down, he knew the Chief had been right. He would take the creature's attention from us, allowing us to escape, and then he would attempt escape himself somehow. After some moments of stillness, he thought it safe to use his penlight. He surveyed the surrounding area. It was indeed a dead end, but he had spotted what appeared to be some sort of trapdoor within the ceiling. Quickly, he pushed open the hatchway and clambored inside.

Now, his thoughts returning to the present, Max had no idea of where he was in relation to his previous location. He knew he had scrambled along the slender tunnel (perhaps some kind of ventilation shaft, though he saw no vents along the side's of the tunnel to confirm his hypothesis) to the left of where he had started, and assumed he was still located within the underground structure that he and Leena had found to be Aztekoth's den, but any further knowledge escaped him.

He had heard no-one following him, earlier or now, and hoped against hope that he had indeed made good his escape. If still within the creature's den, then he had to somehow find his way back to the exit, or find another way out. Either way, while currently safe, he was not yet out of the woods, and he knew it. There was nothing else for it, though. He could not remain where he was, nor was it likely safe to go back the way he had come. So, he continued forward, and hoped he would find what he was looking for.

* * * * * *

The TV was on, the nightly news was announcing the latest happenings during the day within the city, the country, the world; which Sloan usually, strangely, found somewhat soothing. But not tonight. Tonight he barely noticed it was on, barely registered even his wife's presence taking a seat beside him on the couch.

"Bob," his wife said. He'd heard her, of course, for she was right beside him. And yet, it was as though she were a million miles away, so soft and distant did her voice sound to the detective.

"Hey," she said, nudging her husband. "I'm over here."

"Sorry," Sloan said, a little sheepishly. He loved his wife Jane dearly, but tried keeping work away from the family home at all times. Now it seems he'd let his troubles intrude, and he regretted that. "I was just thinking."

"About work?"

"Yeah, but..." He leaned over and gave her a peck on the cheek, "...it's nothing for you to worry about, I promise."

She looked at him with a probing glance, a glance Sloan knew all to well. His wife was a pretty woman of forty five years of age. Somewhat younger than him and, thus far, unaffected by the vagaries of the city, she was nevertheless a strong, forthright woman. She needed to be to be married to a man like Bob Sloan and Sloan himself knew it.

"I know that look, honey, but trust me, it's nothing for you to worry about."

"Bob," Jane said, inching closer to her husband. "Don't shut me out like this. You always keep things so close to your chest, and I usually let it pass at that, but...I can see something is really bothering you this time, and I want you to share it with me."

Sloan stood at this, and marched over to the nearest window. He peered out into the night. It was still raining, and the wind had picked up as well, splashing its presence on the window before him. He hated hurting his wife this way, as he knew he was doing that moment. But he honestly did not know any other course of action to take. There was nothing for him to tell her. He didn't *know* what was wrong with him. And that made it all the harder.

"I wish I could tell you, honey," Sloan said finally, still staring out into the void. "I wish I could tell you."

* * * * * *

The Wraith awoke to find himself in a charnel house, surrounded by the putrefying smell and sight of rotting corpses. Along with an immense headache, it was all he could do to control a strong, gagging influence which now threatened to overwhelm him. He steadied himself as best he could, tried to ignore his surrounds and concentrate. What had happened? He had trouble recalling. He tried standing, but was incredibly shaky on his feet. He leaned up against the nearest wall, attempting to get his bearings and recollect just what had led him there.

Then it all came flooding back. The attempted escape by him and his team, the separation of them in that attempt, and his battle with Aztekoth, which culminated in...

Why am I not dead?

The Wraith puzzled over this. He had been unable to resist the creature's deadly touch, unable to fight, to escape. Death was certain. And yet here he was. Why? He had to know. And had his team managed to get to safety themselves? He yearned to know.

Despite his injuries, his burned face and heavily burned shoulders and upper torso, his powers of recovery were remarkable, and he was again steady on his feet, or as steady as was possible while standing on dozens of decaying cadavers. Every muscle, every fiber of his being ached, but his mind raced, searching for solutions to his current predicament. He inspected his surrounds carefully. Bodies, in varying stages of decomposition, lay everywhere. Rats were in abundance.

Strange, he thought.

There were far more bodies here than had been linked to the serial killings bedeviling the city, killings he now knew Aztekoth to be responsible for. So where did all these bodies come from? There were at least fifty bodies here by his estimation, possibly more, it being difficult to properly ascertain. And he had seen more skeletal warriors at that loathsome ceremony than victims of this recent murder spree. So, the question remained. Judging by the look of the room, akin to that of a dungeon and thusly almost identical to the room he had been imprisoned in earlier, he was still located within Aztekoth's secret underground den.

While the stench was unbearable, The Wraith withstood it and crouched down, inspecting the various remains much more closely. Some had decomposed practically to the bone. Those had been dead for weeks, even months. A thought struck The Wraith. Had Aztekoth and his band resorted to grave robbing? Of removing the recently dead with the aim of removing their hearts for use in their hideous ceremonies? He thought it possible, it would certainly explain the higher number of living dead Aztecs, but he wondered why he hadn't heard of any such act taking place up to that point. Surely it would have made the news? Surely his various snouts would have apprised him of any such situation? It was a puzzle with no answer at present, and now he turned his mind to other matters, namely his escape from this wretched place.

Back on his feet, he made his way across the human flotsam over to the door. It was made of extremely sturdy timber. Old, but in surprisingly good condition, and would not budge under any circumstances. He silently cursed the loss of his belt. What he could do now with the equipment secreted therein...

As if by some miracle, the door suddenly exploded open, sending The Wraith careening to the floor, landing in a heap amongst the bodies and mouldering flesh. Briefly dazed, he shook the cobwebs from his now throbbing skull, to see the smiling and relieved face of Leena looking down at him.

"Darling," she said, quickly helping The Wraith to his feet.

"I'm okay, but we need to get out of here quickly. That blast can't possibly have gone unheard."

Leena nodded her understanding. She led him out of that horrid place and into a dank, musty cavern, wider than the tunnels they had encountered earlier, but no less filthy.

"This way," she whispered, leading the way. The Wraith followed.

The cavern soon darkened, casting the area in an ever-creepier atmosphere. Where the shadows had once lurched along the stone walls, now there was only impending darkness. The Wraith reached up to his temple and pressed at a spot which activated his in-cowl night vision lenses. Leena had undoubtedly done likewise, her lenses were built into her spectacles, for she never broke stride.

In minutes, after climbing a narrow, spiral staircase, they had reached a juncture connecting with the corridor system they had seen earlier.

"We must be careful," The Wraith said under his breath, de-activating his night-vision lenses. "Aztekoth will undoubtedly have guards posted throughout this complex."

"I know the way out. Follow me," Leena replied.

The Wraith continued to follow his partner, as they silently loped through a mix of corridors and passageways.

"I remember where we are now," The Wraith said. "The exit is this way."

Leena stopped him. "No, it's this way."

Perplexed, The Wraith nevertheless allowed Leena to lead them into another darkened walkway. His lenses back in place, the going was tough, trudging through the thick dirt and dust of a tunnel obviously very rarely used in a very long time. That would explain their lack of meeting anyone along the way.

Where on Earth is this place? The Wraith thought to himself.

They were underground, he had long realized that fact, but anything further thus far eluded him.

After a short space of time, the two came out into an expansive, deep grotto, their path opening out onto the top of a high viaduct with large amounts of water spilling through underneath them.

"How did you find this place?" The Wraith said above the noise of the raging torrent below them.

"The Metro City sewer system connects with Aztekoth's underground hideaway at this point. I discovered it when I used a narrower sewer tunnel to escape earlier. The tunnels branch off up ahead, leading to safety."

Inching across the slender causeway, they slipped through an archway and came out into a tunnel of the city's intricate system of sewers.

Then, a shadowy figure emerged from a side-tunnel ahead of them. The Wraith braced himself for action. Into the meek light stepped Max.

"Max, thank heavens," Leena said, embracing the stocky Irishman.

"Good to see you," The Wraith said, taking his hand.

"I sure am glad I found you two. I value my skill at navigating this immense city, but I confess, I was hopelessly lost down here," Max said, breathing an audible sigh of relief.

"Enough for reunions," The Wraith countered. "We need to regroup and reevaluate. We've never before encountered an enemy as powerful as Aztekoth. We need to find a way to stop him, for this city and more will surely fall if we fail."

~ Chapter 12 ~

Back in the comfort of the Lair, Paul felt almost human again. He sat at his great computer terminal, trying to discern any information at all on the creature Aztekoth's origins. His shoulders were heavily gauzed and bandaged, but he barely noticed. When he was on the job, he was focused solely on that, to the detriment of almost everything else.

"Darling?" Leena said.

Paul failed to reply. He was busy reading a detailed article he had found online and heard nothing.

"Paul," Leena said, louder.

"Hmm?" came Paul's vacant reply.

She swiveled him around in his chair so that he was now facing her. Paul was frustrated by this.

"You're injured, you need to be upstairs, resting," Leena said sternly.

"I can't, not while that thing is still out there. We need to know all we can before we can stop it."

"But, we know where its den is located, we can send the army in, wipe Aztekoth and its monsters out in one foul swoop," said Leena.

"No, the creature is no fool," Paul said, standing. "Aztekoth will have contingency procedures in place. It revealed to me how intricate its power base has been weaved already, and I have no doubt its word to be true. As to its den...with our escape, I doubt they will remain there, ready for us to find again. Still, we should alert one of our men to keep the location under surveillance. Perhaps Adam might be available?"

Leena nodded, and Paul knew she would arrange it. Concern then crept into her attractive features. Paul knew that look all too well, and softened somewhat. "Thank you for coming back for me. I'm not sure I would have been able to escape before Aztekoth or one of its warriors had returned. Good job on the Malone case too."

Leena smiled, and Paul knew everything was okay. He knew she'd be off to her day job soon, and didn't want her worrying any more than she had to while there.

"So, what's our next move then?" Leena enquired.

"Well," Paul started, turning back round to face the computer. "While you're contacting Adam, I'll continue with my research here. We need to know more about where Aztekoth came from, and hopefully that may give us some clue as to its weakness, some way that we can overcome it."

Paul again immersed himself in his work, pushing all other considerations from his mind. There had to be a way to defeat Aztekoth, there had to be. And if there were, he would find it. Woe be to this city—this country—if he were to fail!

He was at it for hours, hunched over his computer terminal, reading, researching. In the midst of all this, he received word from Adam that Aztekoth and its warriors had indeed fled from their underground den, the location being deserted upon Adam's arrival. He'd thought as much, but hoped against hope that the creature would be overconfident, careless. He tried to push that disappointment from his mind, and continued with his work.

He rubbed at his eyes. He was exhausted and his shoulders ached. He looked at his Christopher Ward C60 Trident watch. He must have been working for hours, but he couldn't recall what the time had been when he started. It had been morning, now it was late afternoon. Soon, it would be time for his patrols once more. The day had gotten away from him. Still, he'd managed to find several pieces of useful information, though what use that information would be to him in his fight against Aztekoth were at that moment still a mystery to him.

"Have you found anything?" Max said, breaking into Paul's thoughts.

"Hmm? Oh, Max," Paul said, finally noticing the Irishman. "Yes, quite a bit." He took a deep breath before starting. "It appears there was a cult of Aztecs that worshiped the war god Huitzilopochtli to the abandonment of all others. They were feared and mistrusted, even amongst their own kind, for their zeal and cruelty. They were finally cast out from society, shunned but the cult leader—presumably Aztekoth—lead a revolt against their king Montezuma, which ultimately failed. As punishment, those that took part in the attempted coup were buried alive, while the cult leader, for his treachery, was skinned alive, before being buried alongside his followers. Then, as legend has it, a curse was brought down upon the entire cult, their souls damned for all eternity. I can find no further information regarding that though."

"Cursed," Max mused under his breath. "What could that mean? And how could it still be alive after all these centuries?"

"It must have something to do with the stone, otherwise why would Aztekoth want it so badly? And the curse itself...the walking skeletons!"

"You said you saw a beating heart within their ribcages?" Max enquired.

Paul stood, began pacing. "Yes. This resurrected cult is responsible for the recent spate of killings in Metro, which we'd naturally assumed to be the work of a serial killer. The sacrificial rites performed, as well as the hearts themselves, somehow re-animate the bodies of the Aztecs..." He broke off, and quickly sat back down at his terminal.

"What's wrong, Chief?"

"There were more skeletons than murdered victims. I need to find out how that's possible," said Paul before trailing off and ignoring Max's presence. "I need to know more," he softly murmured, and set about investigating his latest idea.

* * * * * *

Sloan was standing in the pouring rain atop the Metro City Police Department. Night had just fallen, though with the weather the way it had been of late, it was often hard to tell. He rubbed the water into his face, then took a look out over the city, a city he had taken such pains to protect time and time again. The sound of the rain drowned out most of the usual city racket, but he could still hear it nonetheless. Home offered no comfort for him now, and the only place he could think of heading to was the station.

The building itself was still fairly new, the previous structure having been destroyed during the Cobra's reign of carnage some time back, but Sloan didn't care much for it. It was new, sure, and it was functional, while the old building had been somewhat damaged from years of neglect. And yet, the old building had character, a soul, that unique quality that was often hard to pin down, let alone enunciate, and it was something this new building of steel and glass just could not match. Thoughts such as these seemed to blacken his mood evermore, and it was then that Sloan truly began to worry. This feeling of dread, of a heaviness on his very soul, had been building for some time, but he'd managed to shake it off, ignore it, each time. It was becoming harder to do, and now he suddenly felt as if all hope were lost, that there was nothing left to fight for. And he was desperate to know why.

Then, he heard a noise behind him—a step into a puddle—and whirled. There stood The Wraith, his cape billowing ominously around him in the wind. In the low light, he looked almost like a creature, demonic and supernatural, and Sloan then realized just what affect The Wraith must have had on the criminal classes.

"Whatta ya want?" Sloan said wearily.

"I have something for you," The Wraith said, as he walked toward Sloan, who remained rooted to the spot by the building ledge.

"I don't want anything from you. You're a vigilante, no better than the rest of the scum out there. Why shouldn't I just arrest you right now?" said Sloan in a belligerent tone.

"I have the truth for you," The Wraith said mysteriously.

Sloan said nothing more, as The Wraith walked up to stand directly in front of the detective. Sloan wanted to grab him there and then, cuff him and take him downstairs to the lockup. He'd wanted to do this for years, had hated all that

The Wraith represented, hated how the vigilante had taken the law into his own hands. And yet, he found himself strangely unable to move, to do anything but watch. The Wraith reached up, and carefully began to remove his cowl from his head. As he did so, the rain drenched a most familiar face, that of Paul Sanderson. And yet, it was somehow even more familiar...

"It's me, Bob. It's Michael."

Sloan jolted, blinked, and then he was alone, the sound of the rain and wind his only companion.

What just happened?

There was no sign anyone else had ever been up there with him tonight, and yet... Had he been hallucinating? Dreaming? He was afraid to admit either, and yet the evidence appeared to point in that direction. A brief wave of nausea enveloped him, as he felt the sweat mingle with the rain running down his face. And then...relief. The blackness infecting his soul had vanished, the almost constant state of worry had gone. The nausea had quickly passed, and what was left was a feeling of exultation. How, why or exactly what had just happened was an absolute mystery to him, but at that moment, he didn't care. But he knew the question, the big question, of what he had just seen or dreamed or hallucinated, would come back to him. And he had no answers.

None at all.

* * * * * *

Paul took the elevator to the upper level of the Lair, headed toward the landing where the various Wraith costumes were located and stored. His intuition had been correct. He had discovered that there had been grave robberies up and down the eastern seaboard, though none in Metro City itself. Not enough in each location to arouse too much suspicion with the local authorities, for there were always some sort of shenanigans going on in cemeteries at night; graffiti, vandalism and the like. But enough, obviously, for Aztekoth to gain the initial numbers it required for its army, along with its victims in Metro. He doubted the authorities would remain in the dark much longer, but had authorized Max to alert them to the dangers they now faced, as Aztekoth could potentially return for more pickings.

A question occurred to him.

Why Metro?

Obviously because of the Cortes Stone. But what exact connection did the stone have with Aztekoth? It's a holy relic, that much was clear, but it had become obvious that the stone itself was the key to the entire mystery. He had to find out why, and he had to find out why Latham had wanted it so badly in the first place. Latham was up to something. Bringing the stone to Metro was not entirely due to his perceived altruism nor his perceived civic pride. He needed answers—tonight.

* * * * * *

Hours later, the rain had died down to a mere trickle, though the wind was still gusting strongly from the north. The Wraith stood atop the city gallery roof, with a canvas backpack carried over his right shoulder, watching the guards below patrolling the grounds. He took a moment to look at the heavens above. No stars were extant, the chunky build-up of clouds was still evident despite the wind, with no respite from the onslaught forecast.

At least the rain has eased for now.

Bringing his mind back to the job at hand, The Wraith next moved backward toward the large glass roof overlooking the main, circular promenade where many of the galleries treasures—especially the Cortes Stone—were located. Before leaving for his nightly patrol, a thought had occurred to him.

If the Cortes Stone is the key to everything, then we need to examine it, study it.

He had told this to Max and Max had been forthright with his replied opinion. He didn't think an examination of it would prove fruitful, certainly not in a quick spate of time. Likely, Latham had already had a barrage of tests carried out, by a field of relevant experts, and whatever secrets the stone had yielded, it would be far easier to extract them from Latham's files—or through the man himself—rather than through an examination of the actual artifact.

Another more important reason, The Wraith had decided, was to ensure that whatever power the stone possessed, to make sure it was not something either Latham or Aztekoth could take advantage of. And the only way to ensure that, was to take the stone, and replace it with a counterfeit.

In the hours prior to The Wraith's arrival there, Max had created a superb likeness, made from plaster and a special plastic resin, of the stone using the futuristic equipment at his disposal in the Lair's laboratory. Photographs and graphs of the stone were in abundance, so while time had been short, Max had nevertheless been able to achieve what had been asked of him. While an expert, at close scrutiny, would likely be able to tell the difference, The Wraith felt sure the counterfeit stone would pass muster for the time being.

The promenade, stretched out below him, was dark and appeared empty. The stone was located within the center, surrounded by the glass case where the Dread Avenger had last seen it. Undoubtedly, Latham would have ensured a flotilla of guards, no doubt just beyond the range of his present sight. The Wraith paused for a moment to consider; the aim was to steal the Cortes Stone, replace it with the counterfeit, and get away without anyone being the wiser.

The Wraith reached to his right temple, pressed at a certain spot, and infra-red lenses dropped into place over the eye-holes in his cowl. He peered down through the glass enclosure, and a myriad of red laser beams—trip alarms— became visible to him. He'd never seen such an array of alarms. Latham truly was doing all he could to protect his precious artifact.

"Chief, I've patched into the gallery mainframe," came Max's voice over his in-cowl communication system. "I'll be able to switch off all alarms in two minutes for a period of five minutes. I can't risk you being discovered if I keep them down any longer."

"Good work, Max," The Wraith whispered. "That will be more than enough time. Standing by."

A beeping over his comm-device indicated it was now or never, and The Wraith quickly acted, opening the service window within the skylight with his trusty lockpick and lowering himself down to the promenade floor via his grapnel and line. There were no guards currently in sight, but The Wraith knew they had to be in the vicinity. Reaching into his belt, he produced his re-breather and a series of cylindrical pellets. With the re-breather secured in his mouth, he tossed the pellets throughout the entire promenade, setting off a thin milky, mist. The Wraith marveled at Max's ingenuity. The gas, Max's latest innovation, would render anyone breathing its fumes completely unconscious, inducing complete amnesia of the two-to-three hours prior to their blacking out. The Wraith thought it best to keep his presence an absolute secret, and this ensured such an outcome.

The Wraith hurried over to the enclosed Cortes Stone. He opened the display case carefully, picking the lock with relative ease.

No alarm. Good.

He held the true stone in his left hand, while reaching into his bag with his right to procure the forgery. He briefly compared the two. To the naked eye, they were identical, right down to the jade embossing around the stone's outer rim. The Wraith could not help but again marvel at Max's skill and ingenuity in creating such a marvel. He only hoped that the forgery would escape detection just long enough to defeat Aztekoth and thwart whatever nefarious plans Latham had. Only then would he return the stone to the museum.

The forgery now in place on the pedestal, The Wraith quickly and carefully replaced the glass cover, locking it into position, and sprinted for his grapnel, which he left in place on the promenade floor. The gas was beginning to dissipate, and the alarm would soon be re-activated. He had to hurry. De-pressing the button on the grapnel device, The Wraith was shot upwards toward the huge skylight. Swiftly climbing up out onto the roof, he re-latched the service door just in time to hear Max's announcement of the alarm coming back online.

The beginnings of dawn were starting to crawl up over the city skyscrapers—murky, gloomy, but nevertheless evident. The Wraith clutched at his bag carefully, for his bounty was a precious and dangerous one. Despite his given opinion, Max would still likely undertake certain tests on the stone. More importantly, however, was that the stone would now be out of the hands of two of The Wraith's deadliest enemies. And for the moment, that was enough.

~ Chapter 13 ~

In almost complete darkness, the creature Aztekoth stood amongst his skeletal brethren, now ranking in the dozens, their faces and forms visible only by torchlight. With shadows and light dancing upon their ebony countenances, Aztekoth paced amongst them.

"We have been forced even further below the earth, beneath our underground den, into this hole as though we are vermin," Aztekoth said. "But no matter. Nothing can stop my plans now." He shifted around to face them. "Time grows short, however. The Wraith and the accursed Robert Latham have delayed us. We must have an army to take this city—and the stone—by force. I weary of this torment. The moment of our salvation will soon be at hand. Tonight, when the moon is at its zenith, I will speak the incantation, and the dead will rise again, and our army will move. The glories of the Aztec Empire will be re-born and with it every one of us will be free of this affliction!"

The murmurings of the gathered Aztecs, both alive and undead, began to build momentum. Aztekoth raised his arms to quell the excitement.

"We will wait here until the sun sets," he announced. "Then we will gather upstairs in the great hall once again, for the final sacrifice will be the start of a whole new order, one that can never be rendered asunder."

Aztekoth bathed in the resultant applause. Soon there would be no further need for hiding. Soon they would overwhelm the entire city, and then the time would come to take back the stone, to regain their forms. The curse would be lifted and the Aztec Empire would take its place as the rightful rulers of this land. Aztekoth rubbed his hands together.

Yes, soon...

* * * * * *

Sloan rubbed his hand through his slightly thinning, dark brown hair. It was early, and he was already seated at his desk at the station. He hadn't slept at all the night before. He didn't need to. He found himself re-energized in a way he hadn't thought possible. The old spring in his step he thought long gone had returned; the feeling of helplessness, of mental exhaustion, now expunged. And what of the hallucination he experienced? He could explain none of it, nothing at all. All he knew was that he felt *good*, better than he had for a long time. And the question raised by that hallucination was somehow behind it.

Michael Reeve alive? Impersonating Paul Sanderson? Is The Wraith?

It was too much to contemplate, and yet, it was something that proved strangely comforting to him. And despite the lack of proof, he knew it to be true. He just *knew*. Now, the mere thought or mention of the name "Wraith" no longer provoked such intense feelings within him. It was as though everything was right with the world.

"Penny for your thoughts?" said Perez, who had just appeared by his desk.

"Nothing important," Sloan replied, smiling. Perez cocked an eyebrow.

"You okay? You seem...different somehow."

Sloan couldn't help but smile again. "I just feel better is all. Resolved a few things."

"Hmm...whatever it is, can I have some? I'm starting to feel as gloomy as this weather. You think it's ever going to stop raining?"

"Climate change, that's what they say," Sloan said, standing. "Nothing we can do about it except ride with it. Anyway, I like the rain. Cleans the muck off."

Sloan eyed Perez carefully, and noted that she appeared tired, listless, and wondered briefly if she were feeling as he had previously.

"Sloan, Perez, get in here!" cried Commissioner Harrison from his office.

They acquiesced, congregating in Harrison's relatively cramped office.

"We're getting reports in from up and down the coast," Harrison began, "of mass grave robberies."

"What?" Sloan said, incredulous.

"Stealing dead bodies?" asked Perez.

"That's exactly what I said," Harrison said. "Cities and towns all along the coast have experienced the same problem. I received a tip this morning and followed through with it."

"From The Wraith?" Sloan probed.

"If you must know..." Harrison started.

"Say no more, I'm okay with it," Sloan said, raising his hands.

Both Harrison and Perez eyed him keenly but said nothing.

"Why are we only hearing about this now?" Perez enquired pointedly. "I mean, something like this in such a widespread area can't have happened purely overnight?"

"You're right. But if you look into it, as I have, the robberies have been over a wide area, but never to excess in any one location. Whoever is responsible has really covered their tracks. We're only now beginning to uncover the enormity of the situation."

"What's the extent of the damage here in Metro?" Sloan queried.

"None. None at all."

Sloan straightened. "Nothing? No bodies stolen? So, we're the lone hold out?"

"So it seems. Another reason why we haven't heard anything up 'til now," Harrison said.

"Why has Metro been spared?" Sloan questioned.

"That's what I want you two to find out," Harrison announced. "Metro appears to be the hub of all the weirdness going on lately, and I want to get to the bottom of this. I've already spoken with the mayor and he's approved my idea."

"Idea?" said Perez.

"You two will be heading the new task force I'm setting up. What with these recent serial killings, now Aztekoth and these grave robberies...we're under-staffed and over-worked as it is. This task force will give us extra manpower and extra funding. Now all we need to do is get out there and catch some bad guys," Harrison outlined. "I'm still working on the details, but just know this: I want action, and I want it fast. I will not tolerate any further crap in my city!"

Sloan and Perez exited Harrison's office and headed back toward Sloan's desk. He plopped down in his chair.

"I don't know about you, but I'm thinking all these recent crimes are related," he said.

"Related? How? We have a spate of serial killings here in Metro, most likely connected to some sort of satanic cult; we have a monster who appears and tears up the city gallery, killing a security guard in the process and now we have a case of body snatchers. How can they be in any way related?"

"Bear with me here," Sloan said, as he leaned forward in his chair, his elbows propped up on his desk. "The first and last of those two could clearly be connected. A satanic cult wanting bodies for its ceremonies. Graves being robbed. Put two and two together."

"I see where you're going there," Perez said. "But what of Aztekoth?"

"I don't think we're really after a satanic cult after all, Perez. I think Aztekoth is behind all this. Somehow, some way, everything leads back to that creature."

"Now all we need is proof," Perez said, taking a seat on the edge of Sloan's desk.

"Well, that's what this task force will be all about. Finding proof and nabbing the culprits. Let's get started."

* * * * * *

Paul sat in the antique brown wing chair within his study library, brooding over a cup of Earl Grey tea. As he took a sip of the pleasant, sweet bergamot-flavored liquid, he pondered all that had happened thus far. It was a case of incredible intensity, and the potential dangers they faced were astronomical. Still, unless further answers were obtained from an examination of the Cortes Stone, nothing could be done until and unless Aztekoth decided to show himself. The next move belonged to the creature, and that fact alone scared Paul beyond measure.

As his thoughts drifted, Paul noticed a flash from the corner of his eye. Looking down at his watch, he noted the CW logo flashing a distinct yellow—Max was calling from the Lair. When an operative was attempting contact from elsewhere, his watch's logo would flash red instead.

Pulling the remote control device to open the door to the Lair from his trouser pocket, Paul moved swiftly through the opened door and into the small, circular elevator. In mere moments he was by Max's side in the laboratory.

"This piece is amazing, I've been at it all day," Max reported eagerly.

"Have your studies yielded any results?"

"Some, though nothing I could not have found by hacking into Latham's files. Which I did. The stone itself possesses power of incredible magnitude. Touching it without protective clothing is deadly. That was found out by the team Latham had hired to procure it in the wilds of Mexico and again here in Metro, when Bartholomew Gregory fell victim to the stone," Max said.

"Now we know why he wasn't at the unveiling," Paul said under his breath. "Did you ascertain exactly what happened?"

"Much the same as what happened to that poor guard at the hands of Aztekoth. Gregory died violently after touching the stone, not long after delivery of it at the gallery, and in front of several witnesses. Apparently he acted as though in some kind of trance, though I've yet to see any evidence of the stone's ability to do this personally."

Paul paced a bit before speaking. "Anything else?"

"Nothing I myself have discovered through personal examination. The stone is, obviously, aged and perfectly legitimate. It's a beautiful specimen, but I have no idea how to gauge or harness the power it obviously possesses."

"Be careful, it's clearly quite dangerous. Keep checking Latham's files for any further data. Lock the stone away for now, we don't want to unwittingly unleash forces we don't yet comprehend. The fact that it's safely stored here, away from either Latham or Aztekoth, is enough for now. Aztekoth wants the stone, needs it for some purpose crucial to his plans, and until the creature is dealt with, I don't intend anyone having it."

* * * * * *

As soon as night had fallen, the legion of Aztecs gathered once again in the great hall of their underground den. In moments, the creature Aztekoth had appeared before them, ready to deliver on his promise of liberation. Two burly Indians also appeared, dragging along another pitiable victim of their devilry. A portly man with thinning, grey locks struggled as best he might under such circumstances. The terror on his face was palpable as he was confronted with the sights of the walking dead around him.

"Tonight begins a new era," Aztekoth roared. "With this final sacrifice, an army will arise from their graves, and with it, the salvation of the empire will finally be realized. After more than half a millenia, our torment will soon be at an end. And we will re-build. Yes, we will re-build what was lost, what was taken from us and there will be vengeance. Vengeance against all those who disbelieve. Vengeance against all those who would deny us life and power. Our great god Huitzilopochtli will bless us and give us the power to create an empire in his name!"

With the poor victim, gagged as he was, now forced to his knees before Aztekoth, the creature bent down, his hollow eyes burning a fiery red.

"Feel no fear, for you are about to become a part of something far greater than your pitiful life," Aztekoth said, his eyes strobing intensely. "Your sacrifice will enable an entire empire to be re-born!"

The victim began to calm, soothed somehow by Aztekoth's words, brainwashed by the light from its eyes.

"Find peace in the knowledge that your sacrifice will enable your betters to live. The greater good is paramount!"

In moments, the victim was secured to the altar, and a robust Indian supplied Aztekoth with an ornate, jade encrusted poniard.

"Behold, as I begin the incantation..." Aztekoth moaned, plunging the dagger into the victim's chest, violently cutting and tearing at the flesh, smashing through the ribcage as though they it was rotten wood. In amongst the morass of free-flowing blood, the organ was procured. Aztekoth held it aloft in triumph. "With this heart, I call upon the great Huitzilopochtli, to grant life to another of our fallen. Then we will have resurrected the fifty, and an army can be born!"

Aztekoth carried the bloodied organ over to the side of the stage, where another shabby crate was located. An Indian ripped the lid off with his bare hands, revealing an ancient skeletal form, covered in centuries of dust and cobwebs. Moaning in ancient Aztec, the creature gently laid the still beating heart on top of the body's ribs and watched as the organ seemed to liquify, seeping through before solidifying in place where the ancient warrior's heart once beat. Within a minute, the long-dead Aztec was standing alongside its progenitor, supplied with its armory, and escorted to join its kin.

Aztekoth returned to the central area of the stage, where he was met by one of its heavy-set Indians, who nodded. Aztekoth indicated his understanding.

"There has been a breaking in the weather. The sky is clear and the moon is full," Aztekoth began in ancient Aztec. "Now I beseech thee, Huitzilopochtli! Show us your power. Raise an army that will be worthy of you, that will be true only to you! Raise an army to bring life to our long-dead empire, and I will raise a temple to you higher than anything this planet has seen. Hear me, o great one, grant us this wish, bring to life this city's dead and I will ensure the cult of Aztekoth will rule in your name for all eternity!"

With that, the large congregation erupted into an orgy of cries and almost rioting, such was the excitement, the level of expectation, the realization that a centuries long wait was nearly at an end.

Aztekoth raised his arms for silence, and after some minutes, silence was achieved.

"It is done."

* * * * * *

Paul spent the early part of the evening working out before heading out for his usual patrol of the city streets. He'd stayed home a little longer than was his norm as Leena was working a late shift that night at the library and he wanted to speak with her in person before heading out.

He pushed himself hard, lifting a multitude of heavy weights, punching the bag with as much power as he could muster, and testing the limits of his gymnastic prowess on the rings, pommel and balance beam. He found a good workout in the Lair's fully equipped gym often helped clear his mind, to help clarify his thoughts. There was much on his mind, and the fact that very little progress had been possible to apprehend those responsible for some of the most heinous crimes imaginable grated at his very soul.

"Chief, there's trouble, major trouble," Max said, rushing into the gym.

Paul ceased his workout immediately, looked gravely at his right-hand man. "What is it? What's wrong?"

"Leena's just gotten off work. She's frantic," he said, not making much sense.

"What's happening?" Paul demanded.

"She's reported from the library parking lot. There's hundreds of 'em, marching down the street."

"Who? What?"

"Zombies. The living dead are streaming through the streets of Metro City!"

~ Chapter 14 ~

Leena had been right. There they were, marching through the streets, causing mayhem wherever they went. Zombies. Their decaying corpses re-animated he knew not how, but now was not the time to ponder such puzzles. He dropped his mini-binoculars back into its pouch in his belt.

It was time for action.

"Darling."

Atop their rooftop vantage point, The Wraith and Max turned. There was Leena, outfitted in the skintight outfit she usually wore when on duty with the Dread Avenger.

"The situation is grave," The Wraith said. "The entire inner city appears inundated with these...things."

"Have the authorities been notified?" Leena queried, taking a look down into the streets.

"Yes, and I've heard a lock-down of the city will take place," The Wraith explained. "S.W.A.T. should be here shortly, and the regular forces are just arriving now."

As The Wraith spoke, sirens could be heard approaching, and the three saw several police cars zig-zagging through the sparse traffic and the morass of bodies crammed into such limited space. One car slammed into a series of zombies, only to find that they simply stood back up and continued on their way.

"What's their purpose? And how can they be stopped? They appear invulnerable," Leena uttered.

"I guess you can't hurt the dead," Max said.

"We have to try," The Wraith said, reaching to his belt, producing his grapnel device and firing it. With the line attached to an overhanging street light, he leaped over the edge of the building, swinging down toward street level, leaving Max and Leena alone with their thoughts.

* * * * * *

Sloan and Perez sprang from their unmarked, their guns raised as they hunched down behind their car.

"Jeez, what is going on here, Perez?" Sloan said, his voice raised. "What are these things? Where did they come from?"

"Your guess is as good as mine, though from the looks of them, I think I can guess," she replied.

They watched and waited, as the zombies simply marched on through the streets, doing nothing more than cause chaos with what little traffic there still was. Cops had arrived, trying to direct traffic and rein in the building army of the living dead, but without much luck.

"What can we do, Bob?"

"Wait for S.W.A.T. and watch. Be careful," he said, as some zombies came perilously close to their position.

Then, from nowhere, the zombies reacted, and suddenly became violent. They began smashing store windows, attacking nearby cars (and their occupants) and anything that moved, causing mayhem with every opportunity.

"Holy crap! They're rioting," Sloan said, as he fired some rounds from his .48, capping a few of the zombies. Those that were hit recoiled slightly, but simply carried on as though nothing had happened—and now they were headed their way.

"Oh shoot," Sloan uttered. He staggered to his feet, and started wailing on the zombies. Perez fired her piece, but it was no use, the bullets had no effect whatsoever save to bring further attention onto themselves. She resorted to hand-to-hand combat as well.

"Hit 'em hard, they're not super strong. Take no prisoners," Sloan shouted.

For a while, they held their own. Both Sloan and Perez were experienced police officers, trained in various forms of combat. The bodies of the zombies proved to be weak, no doubt due to the length of time of their internment.

As the detectives continued to fight for their survival, the number of zombies approaching kept growing. Their rotting forms could no longer hold up during battle, but their number proved too great, and before much longer, Sloan and Perez began to tire. The living dead began to overwhelm them.

"Perez," Sloan cried out desperately. But she had already gone under, her body covered with those of their attackers. It was too late. All was lost. Then, as if from nowhere, he heard it. The sound of salvation.

"Filthy denizens from Hell," came a familiar voice. "Go back from whence you came!"

Sloan managed to catch sight of The Wraith, launching himself into the meleé with a swiftness and power.

The Wraith stormed in with a ferocity unlike anything Sloan had ever seen before. He was just one man and yet he fought with the power and vigor of a dozen. He had seen The Wraith in battle before, knew how skilled he was in hand-to-hand combat, but this was something else. It was as though the Dread Avenger was some medieval warrior, fighting for all there was with everything he had. And more.

Despite the incredible odds, The Wraith managed to free Sloan, yanking him to his feet and scattering four zombies at the same time. Grabbing two more of the undead and throwing them aside, he was able to free Perez as well.

"We have to get out of here, regroup," Sloan panted, while The Wraith battled on ferociously.

The Wraith continued his onslaught , producing a small metallic object from a pouch on his belt. At the press of a button, it instantly enlarged into a long bow staff. With a cry, he plowed into the crowd of zombies surrounding them, knocking off their heads, impaling others, taking out the legs beneath the knees of others. The battle continued, with the three of them fighting on with as much strength as they could muster.

Soon, they were free from immediate danger, the zombies that had attacked them lying at their feet in piles of decomposing flesh. Sloan cocked an eye down the street: there were more headed their way, and he knew even with The Wraith by their side, they couldn't take all of them.

"Agreed," The Wraith said finally. "We'll head for higher ground." He pointed to a nearby rooftop. The Dread

Avenger sprinted for the building's entrance; Sloan and Perez followed swiftly behind.

* * * * * *

The three stormed onto the adjacent rooftop. The Wraith perched himself on the building ledge; Sloan and Perez approached him from behind.

"It's an invasion," The Wraith said. "The entire city is being swarmed. We need the national guard, the army."

"S.W.A.T.'s on their way, should be here shortly. National Guard is a day or two away," Sloan explained.

"Not good enough. S.W.A.T. may make some inroads, but they're heavily outnumbered. The regular police force are no match for this. We need to get the people out and contain these monsters to within the inner city. We cannot let them break free," The Wraith said.

"But how? What can we do?" Perez asked, somewhat frantic, her nerves still clearly frazzled.

"You need to get some rest, possibly some medical attention," The Wraith told Perez. "And you, get to police headquarters, push the authorities there to get the armed forces here as quickly as possible. The powers that be need to know this is a necessity above all others."

"Right," Sloan said with an eager friendliness. The Wraith noted this and briefly wondered why the change in attitude. "What will you do?"

"Anything I can." And with that, The Wraith sprinted forth, leaping from that rooftop to one adjacent and quickly onward.

* * * * * *

Leena paced atop their rooftop vantage point alongside Max, who watched the zombies rioting in the streets below. She and Max had tried combating the zombies, but had quickly discovered how outnumbered they were, and subsequently retreated to safety. Just how long they could remain safe up there, she could only wonder. The zombies were just as capable as reaching their location as anyone else.

"We need reinforcements. Badly," The Wraith said behind her, causing her to whirl around.

"Darling," Leena said, falling into his arms.

"The entire city will soon fall unless prompt action is taken. We need to get the people out, what few remain at this hour, and ensure the zombies stay in."

"How do we achieve that?" Max enquired.

"If we can get S.W.A.T. involved in this, perhaps the regular police with enough firepower as well, they might be able to establish control lines at key locations, then perhaps we can hold those lines until the National Guard or army arrive," The Wraith said.

"Army? Holy—" Max uttered. "But can we hold them that long?"

"If we can hold out at least a day, that will at least give the army a chance to get here. In the meantime, we'll have to do all we can and hope it's enough. The zombie numbers are too great. We need men and we need firepower. Once S.W.A.T. arrives, we can chop them down causing as little overall damage to the city as possible in the process."

"Here they are," Max said, nodding toward street level. Indeed, there was a flotilla of trucks arriving, barging through the zombies, emptying their cargo of heavily armed officers onto the street and taking down the living dead where they saw them.

The Wraith stepped up to the ledge. "Good. I need to get down there, find the officer in charge, help coordinate the control efforts. We're fighting a war here, one we cannot afford to lose."

~ Chapter 15 ~

"We need control lines set up at George, 35th, MacGregor and Hirst Streets," The Wraith barked, pointing at each key location on a map provided by the S.W.A.T. commanding officer. "We may need to shift positions if the situation changes."

The commanding officer nodded in agreement. Together, they went through the men and handpicked which man went to which location, spreading them out as much as possible along each perimeter. Weaponry and ammunition were spread out evenly, ensuring each man had ample supply. Barricades were rigged as best they could, for time was of the essence and no-one knew how long this lull would last. The Wraith and his newfound partner moved around, inspecting as many of the control lines as they could. The urban soldiers were stationed, their bodies tensed, gripping their weapons tightly, ready for the defense of the city, ready to fight for their very lives.

The Wraith took his position at the location he thought most likely to see action first. He stood, his muscles contracted, ready for action. He watched and waited. Down the street, a crowd of zombies began slowly building up once more. A few moments more and they began their rampage, some marching, others sprinting, toward their position. At The Wraith's command, the surrounding officers fired with powerful machines guns and shot guns, cutting the zombies off at the knees, halting their progress. As though they understood, the zombies would then retreat, back to where they started at the far end of the street, before re-gathering and slowly building up their numbers once more.

Again and again, the zombies would re-establish their forces. Again and again they would charge in large numbers, only to be forced back by violent gunfire.

The Wraith and his men were barely holding their lines. The numbers of the marching dead were ever-increasing, and it became obvious that without breaking off the line of their entry into the city, they would not be able to hold out with their limited ammunition until reinforcements were due to arrive, and nobody knew when that would be.

The Dread Avenger noticed Sloan and Perez had returned. Perez had a bandage around her head. "We need to find their point of entry into the city. We cut them down in the hundreds and they keep coming back in increasing numbers.".

Sloan nodded in agreement and moved over to the commanding officer, speaking into his ear. In moments, with a handful of officers in tow, the three of them raced off in two unmarked police cars to find the zombies' entry point into the city. Deep down, the Dread Avenger hoped there wouldn't be much of the dead left. Too many, and they would have next to no hope of cutting them off, let alone holding out until the army might arrive.

Thankfully, there were still areas of the inner city seemingly unoccupied by the zombies, which made travel all the easier. Occasionally they would come across patches of the undead, which they would take down with their cars and their onboard weaponry. As they traveled around the inner city and its outskirts, they were unable to detect any site of entrance the zombies had taken. Were they now within the city confines in their entirety? The Wraith doubted this, for as many zombies as they had thus far encountered, there would undoubtedly be more dead in a city as immense as Metro. He wondered briefly how Leena and Max were faring. He had assigned them watch duty, to keep track of the zombies' movements and activities from higher ground and to alert him if anything terrible happened. So far, he hadn't heard from either of them, but knew better than to be worried.

While he was thinking, hoping that the authorities had been able to evacuate the public from the city as per his directives, he was interrupted.

"There!" Sloan suddenly cried out from the passenger seat.

The Wraith, piloting Sloan's unmarked, averted his attention and saw the steady march of the undead streaming down Edgeworth Avenue, one of the main thoroughfares leading into the city from the west.

This was it, where they must make their stand.

The Wraith slammed his foot on the brake; the car spun sharply to the right as it came to rest at the side of the road. The other car stopped alongside them.

"We must cut them off here," The Wraith told them. "We need to give the authorities back in the city the best possible chance of holding out the zombies by stopping the zombies' line of entry here. We *must* prevail."

"But, we don't have enough firepower to hold them for long," Perez countered.

Sloan looked to her then to The Wraith, who permitted a rare moment to smile.

"I don't intend *holding* them here. I intend on destroying them!" The Wraith said.

With that, the Dread Avenger directed the group of eight to positions at the junction of Edgeworth and Elstree Street. Weaponry at the ready, they fired at The Wraith's command, cutting the zombies down with ferocious power. The procession up ahead made no move to fall back and attack, while the zombies pouring into the city from the west simply kept coming, allowing The Wraith and the others to create a gap with which they were able to establish a beachhead from where they were able to press their attack at the mindless creatures storming toward them.

"There's no end to them," Sloan yelled. "We're gonna run outta bullets eventually."

The Wraith knew he was right, but knew also that he had weaponry of his own to take out far more zombies than even a machine gun could. He reached down to his belt and pulled from it several small red capsules. The Wraith allowed himself another brief smile. *Red for danger*, Max had told him. Danger indeed.

"What's that?" Sloan asked.

The Wraith ignored him and lobbed a few of the capsules into the path of the oncoming horde. On contact with the ground, they ignited in a fiery inferno. Not an explosion per sé, for there was next to no noise and no destructive force. Instead, intense flames shot up from the ground, engulfing those in its path. In moments, those caught were consumed utterly, their ashes the only evidence of their having existed at all.

"Whoa!" Sloan managed to utter.

The Wraith repeated this maneuver, tossing pellets with pinpoint accuracy, the tiny red bombs of death landing at the feet of the myriad approaching zombies, with the same result as before. In combination with the continuing barrage from Sloan and his team, they were finally making some headway in their war against this army of the living dead. He hadn't used the pellets earlier, not until he had fully assessed the enemy, their capabilities and their weaknesses. With limited quantities, he had to use the capsules at just the proper time and place.

It was a slaughter. As scores of undead kept coming toward them, The Wraith and his team threw everything they had at the zombies. Rotting flesh was torn apart by gunfire, whole bodies were rendered asunder by flash pellets. As the massacre continued, The Wraith knew they had to be precariously close to running out of ammunition against such a vast enemy, and his supply of incendiary capsules had just about been exhausted as well.

"They're thinning out," Sloan shouted above the noise of battle. "We're winning!"

It was true. The procession of zombies flooding in from the west had begun to thin to a mere trickle.

In smaller numbers, they continued mindlessly towards them, Sloan and the rest cut them down with relative ease, while The Wraith used the last of his flash capsules to do likewise. Then it was over.

"Just in time, too," Sloan said, wiping his brow. "We'd just about run out of bullets."

The Wraith placed both hands on the detective's shoulders; Sloan only smiled in reply. There was clearly a mutual understanding there, one The Wraith did not yet understand.

Next, he examined what they'd wrought. There were decomposing bodies and body parts strewn everywhere. The stink of the dead sat thick in the air. Metro City had truly become a war zone.

"Let's barricade Edgeworth. Drive our cars across here" — The Wraith pointed— "and here. We'll need to commandeer those cars over there as well. Block this main thoroughfare into the city with as much as we can find, just in case any more of those creatures appear."

"We'll need to call for backup, at least so we can re-stock on ammunition," Perez said.

"Do it. Tell them to double-check the main access points into the city. Hold the line here until they arrive. I'll head back to the city, help in any way I can," The Wraith replied.

He turned and peered back toward the inner city, which loomed over and around him ominously. They'd won a major battle here...but only just. He knew deep down that the odds were still stacked heavily against them, with likely thousands more zombies cramming into the confines of Metro, wreaking carnage in their wake. Could the police force manage to hold their own?

Aztekoth would pay for this, The Wraith vowed to himself. Oh there would be vengeance, such as this city had never before seen.

"I swear it," he said.

* * * * * *

With S.W.A.T. onsite, the police were able to hold their own—barely. Their added firepower and combat skills certainly came in handy at that point. But could they hold out long enough? Could they prevail against such overwhelming odds, against such an adversary?

Leena, watching the butchery from a nearby rooftop, was roused from such thoughts by Max, who was standing alongside her and who she'd just noticed was talking into the tiny Bluetooth earpiece in his left ear.

"Right, Chief. Out."

"What was that all about?" she asked.

"The Chief managed to block the zombies' entry over on the west side. It looks like they're in the city in their entirety now, but there's a lot still headed this way," he reported.

"Looks like thousands are already here, swarming all through the city streets," she said. "We're hopelessly outnumbered, they've only managed to hang on down there because those monsters are mindless, just aimlessly lumbering back and forth. But sooner or later..."

"I know," Max said. "But what can we do? Apart from the few weapons we have at our disposal—I have a few flash pellets still—I don't see what we can do. And those pellets won't last long. We need to use them wisely."

"I know, I know. But I feel so helpless up here. I need to get down there and do something. I'm watching our city—*our home*—being destroyed before our very eyes. We can't let it end like this!"

Leena hated feeling this way. She always prided herself on her strength and courage, on her independence and forthrightness. But now she felt everything closing in on her. Helplessness, despair...

No, she countered. It wouldn't end this way, not now. She wasn't about to let Aztekoth and his monsters get away with this. There was still some fight in her yet.

"Max," she directed. "Get over to the eastern end of Edgeworth Avenue. Those zombies should still be heading down there. Cut them off as best you can with your flash capsules. Reduce the amount coming toward our forces here. That will hopefully buy them some time at least. Buy *us* some time to think of something more."

"On it," Max said, doffing his cap. He raced off.

Leena looked back down at the massacre occurring on street level. The cops were still managing to hold their line, but she knew this would only be temporary. She hoped Max would be in time to provide his delaying measure. And The Wraith, what of The Wraith? She hoped he'd think of something, and soon. Or all might yet be lost.

* * * * * *

The Wraith raced from rooftop to rooftop. He needed to get back into the inner city, back to help as best he could. Deep down, he knew his effectiveness would be limited. Without flash capsules, with little more than a bow staff and a grapnel and line, he had but his fists and feet. But he would fight, fight to the last drop of blood in his veins. Metro would not fall to the likes of Aztekoth. Not this day.

Aztekoth, he thought. *That fiend has brought such devastation and pain to my city. There will be retribution.*

As he sprinted, he would occasionally peek down into the streets to keep abreast of the zombies movements or for any potential change in their behavior. He followed the course of Edgeworth directly into the city, watching as the procession of the living dead continued forth alongside his path. Suddenly, something street level caught his eye. That man down there...*Max?!* He had to hurry, before it was too late.

Attaching his grapnel and line to a nearby lamp post, he descended as quickly as possible to help his friend in battle. The Dread Avenger landed harshly, though steadily, on the curb. Max was by now hurling flash capsules into the throng of the dead, taking care of several of them at a time. In moments, The Wraith was by his friends side, eager to join the battle.

"Chief!" Max cried.

"Give me some capsules, quickly," The Wraith said.

Max complied, handing the Dread Avenger a sizable portion of his remaining pellets. The two then barged in among the milling horde, tossing capsules to the ground on all sides, causing great casualties amongst the zombie army. With each throw, several of the undead were consumed in flames, destroyed almost instantly. Despite the carnage, they were heavily outnumbered in this part of the city, and their capsules were running out fast. The Wraith knew that, perhaps, he could battle on, that perhaps the Eyes of Judgment may prove an effective delaying tactic, if not quite an offensive weapon. He wasn't sure if it would work against the dead, but it was worth a shot. But what of Max? While his stocky assistant was an able fighter in normal situations, this was hardly normal and he feared for the Irishman's safety.

"I'm running dry here," Max said, confirming The Wraith's worst fears, for he too was down to his last three capsules.

He lobbed another at the feet of three oncoming zombies, utterly consuming them in the subsequent discharge of intense heat. And another at four more, his aim so good as to take them all out with the one throw, the flames shooting up, reducing the dead to ashes. The Wraith noted that the zombies in this section of the city were more attentive to their surroundings, and perhaps slightly less violent. Were these zombies merely scoping out the territory while they continued their rampage? The Wraith could only wonder.

Down to his last flash capsule, The Wraith hurled it, taking another few zombies back to the hell from whence they'd come. He then took his grapnel from his belt, fired it up at a flag pole on the building looming above them, reached over to Max, attached the grapnel gun to the Irishman's belt, and pressed the retract button.

"Good bye, old friend," The Wraith said in the instant before Max, clearly surprised, was yanked upward off his feet to safety.

The Wraith would fight on, of course, but he would not sacrifice his friend in such a helpless cause. If now was the time to die, he would go down alone, while taking as many zombies as he could with him. It's not as though he was giving up the fight overall. That was not his style. But he knew if an evil the likes of Aztekoth were to ever be defeated, men as intelligent, as cunning, as resourceful and loyal as Max Horton would be needed in such a fight. To him, it was an obvious choice to spirit his friend away to fight another day.

The Wraith was now forced to retreat back a few steps, as a large group of zombies began to slowly advance toward him. The look of menace and cruelty on their faces caused the hair his neck to stand on end. He would fight on, to the bitter end, yes. But was this the end? The Wraith cursed that possibility, but as the zombies came ever closer, that possibility seemed increasingly more likely.

* * * * * *

Leena kept watch on the proceedings below. The cops had somehow managed to continue holding their own, but the question nevertheless remained: just how long could they keep that up? She feared the worst. Despite her always strong sense of optimism, she knew full well the potential realities of the current situation. As such dire thoughts went through her brain, the noise of approaching trucks suddenly filled the air. What—or who—was that? Rounding a corner two blocks down from her current location, Leena spotted a bevy of armored vehicles barraging down the boulevard toward the gathered throng of police.

"The National Guard," Leena said aloud, elated. *They've done it*, she thought. *They've broken through!* "We've won!"

"Foolish woman!" a horrific voice came from behind her.

Leena whirled around. Aztekoth stood before her.

"You," she managed to utter, momentarily caught off guard.

"You have won nothing," the creature moaned. "Your tactics have merely delayed the inevitable. This army I have created may be doomed. But there are others, waiting to be re-born. The Aztec empire will reign supreme once more."

Leena stood steadfast. "Not while there is breath in my body!"

"Strong words," Aztekoth said in a mocking tone. "You have neither the power nor the will to withstand me. None of you do."

"I think the current situation says otherwise," Leena snapped back.

Aztekoth laughed with such a guttural, otherworldly tone, that it caused her to briefly shudder. "You of this modern world, you believe yourselves the cradle of civilization, the most powerful in the world. Yet, there are forces beyond your ken. Power you could not possibly dream of. My followers were buried alive for their loyalty to me. My soul was banished to eternal torment within what you know as the Cortes Stone, until the inscription was spoken, releasing me from that living hell, only to find myself shackled to this rotting carcass. Only the stone itself can make me whole once more. I will show this country the meaning of vengeance, of true power. Our empire will rise from the ashes of your city, I will bathe in the blood of my enemies, and your puny nation will cease to exist!"

Leena let her emotions get the better of her. She charged the creature. Knowing not what she would do, but attempting combat all the same, she came at Aztekoth with everything she had. The creature remained impassive, as she swung with a powerful roundhouse punch. Her arm went through thin air. She tried again, this time with a spinning scissor-kick, which would render an ordinary assailant catatonic. The same result.

"You are pitiful," Aztekoth began. ""I spared The Wraith's life earlier so that I may study him. Or perhaps torture him. That proved a mistake. But *you* might prove useful."

Leena didn't like the sound of that, but before she could utter a word in protest, Aztekoth reached a bony arm toward her and a putrefying gas began to seep from the surrounding grimy rags. Darkness beckoned, but in the moments before she fell into unconsciousness, she reached for her Tissot watch, and pressed a button on its side.

Blackness then enveloped her...

~ Chapter 16 ~

The Wraith clenched his jaw.

No, he thought.

Despite the odds, he vowed that today would not be the day of his demise. Pressed up against the wall of an adjacent office building, the zombies loomed ever nearer, expressions of rage and mindless hunger etched upon their emaciated faces. With a half dozen almost upon him, The Wraith unleashed his Judgment Stare on the hapless horde.

"Halt!" he boomed, the Eyes of Judgment crackling with a fierce, otherworldly energy. "Your march on this city is over. Your purpose is at an end. I send you back to the depths of Hell from whence you came!"

The Wraith had gambled that perhaps, just perhaps, he might be able to influence the zombies' behavior through the power of the Eyes of Judgment. So far, they had stopped in their tracks. Now they were acting as though confused or even lost.

"Be gone!" The Wraith bellowed.

The expressions on the rabble had changed. Enveloped with the energies of the Eyes of Judgment, they no longer appeared vicious, savage. Now they were only figures to be pitied. Helpless souls that had somehow been resurrected, of a sort, to do the bidding of a creature whose evil knew no boundaries. And now, due to the powers of The Wraith's Judgment Stare, it was as though they had seen the truth of their situation, the truth of their so called benefactor, Aztekoth. And they could not handle it.

"BE GONE!" The Wraith intoned once again.

The assembled horde before him now began to quiver in unison, which quickly turned into a violent shaking.

The Wraith watched on as the zombies began to fall apart, their very bodies crumbling, ultimately falling to dust at his feet and in the street immediately in front of him. The assemblage further ahead remained standing, though now no longer marching further into the city and looking equally as lost as the others had only moments before.

The Wraith stood a moment, perplexed. Could the Eyes of Judgment had somehow affected the others not within its proximity? Were the zombies, therefore, linked somehow, mentally? He couldn't fathom how this could be possible, and yet, there was so much he had experienced recently that was seemingly beyond the realms of possibility. Yet here they were.

Suddenly, the remaining zombies began shaking as the others had earlier. And, finally, they succumbed to whatever malady the Eyes of Judgment had inflicted upon them. The battle was over. He had won. There was no time for internal congratulations, however. He knew not if the other zombies still attacking the inner city would likewise be affected, so he needed to get over there as quickly as possible. He would re-group with Max and the police and S.W.A.T. to deal, if need be, with the remaining hordes of the living dead as best they could. But now, at least, they had a weapon proven effective in combat.

The Eyes of Judgment had surprised the Dread Avenger much of late. He found he was still discovering new ways to utilize the power he had been blessed with. He briefly wondered if there were any limits to this power. Before he could ponder this question further, the distress beacon on his Christopher Ward C60 Trident watch buzzed. Removing his gauntlet, he saw the orange flashing of the CW logo on the watch face. Orange meant that Leena was now contacting him. She was in some sort of danger and needed urgent help.

A dilemma. Should he race to her rescue or join Max and the police as he had originally intended? As much as he loved her, he knew she would understand that the greater good, the city and its people, had to come first. He rushed to find Max. Several issues needed their focus, and the sooner they saw to those, the sooner they could turn their attention toward Leena. He only hoped that they wouldn't be too late.

* * * * * *

The incessant humming was beginning to give Leena a throbbing headache.

"Mmmmf...keep it down," she mumbled.

Then she felt the pain flooding through her arms and legs. Full consciousness now came to her, and she realized the deep peril of her situation. She was trussed up tightly on a giant X-shaped crucifix, her arms and legs spread out, harshly tied to each of the rotted wooden posts. The thick cords bit into her flesh. She struggled against her bonds. No movement. None.

She forced herself to take control of her emotions. *Don't panic*, she thought. *Don't let the situation overwhelm you.*

The humming was coming from behind her. She craned her neck to try and get a look; it was impossible. From the noise, it was obvious there were a great many people there. She looked above and around her, now fully taking in her surroundings. She was back in Aztekoth's underground lair. Or perhaps a different, albeit similar in appearance, location? She could not be sure. Irrespective of her location, and despite her training and experience fighting by the Dread Avenger's side...she was afraid.

"You have awoken," Aztekoth said, emerging from the distant shadows as though he was one with the darkness. "Good. I will derive great pleasure in committing your sacrifice while you are conscious."

The sounds of wood-on-wood now filled the immense chamber, as the humming increased in intensity, reaching such a level as to almost drown out Leena's own thoughts.

Aztekoth raised his hideous arms, and the assembled group, no doubt the creature's footsoldiers, began to die down a little. "Your heart will raise my queen. Then we will render our army anew, and this city will finally fall so that the Aztec Empire can be reborn!"

The horde raised their voices in loud unison once again, while Leena struggled valiantly against her bonds, but to no use.

"Struggle not, my child, for you are about to give the gift of life to a true believer, to one whom was so wronged. My beloved..." Aztekoth's voice drifted away slightly, as though he was remembering a moment in his past. Leena noted this, but the moment passed and the creature resumed his sinister purpose.

"The time is now at hand," he began, beckoning to his followers. "Your queen will rise again, to sit at my side as we resurrect our lost empire. And then, as our flock has increased in number, we will take back the Cortes Stone, and we will be whole once more."

A raucous cry rose up, coupled with claps and much tapping of wood-on-wood. Leena remembered what Aztekoth had told her earlier. It came to her just how important the stone was to him. Not just because it was a relic sacred to the Aztecs. Not just because its resting place had been desecrated by Latham's crew. It had somehow been Aztekoth's tomb up until a member of Latham's expedition read aloud the inscription upon it, releasing the creature, restoring him to some semblance of life. Aztekoth needed the stone, needed to use its immense power to somehow restore himself and his followers to proper human form.

Incredible, Leena thought. Paul had been right in his theory of the stone's importance. If only he was here now. If only there was some way for her to escape.

She struggled again with her bonds, which remained as tight as ever, the cords biting evermore into her flesh. Blood trickled down her arms. She attempted to internalize the pain, to force it into a small corner of her brain that she could lock away. Paul had taught her that technique, though it was often easier said than done.

"Behold, my people," Aztekoth moaned. "The obsidian knife, which has helped bring new life to our people, will be used again."

He held the knife aloft. Leena knew the end was coming. As the creature slowly glided toward her, her only regret was that she had been unable to make her relationship with Paul truly official. Oh, they were a couple to the world, true enough. But deep down, she yearned for marriage, a final commitment. Even with her world filled with such dangers and horrors no one could possibly imagine, and despite the fulfillment she felt in her life, and that which Paul and her job gave her, she nevertheless wanted what so many other people wanted—love, happiness, a family. Paul, in his life as Michael Reeve prior to becoming The Wraith, had always wanted such a life, while she had rebelled. Now it was almost as if it was the other way around.

Funny, she thought, *how often people say their lives flash before them at the moment before death.* She was experiencing that sensation at that very moment.

With Aztekoth looming larger and larger, she shut her eyes. She had no wish for her last vision in this world to be of such horror.

She waited grimly for the end.

An explosion ripped through the immense hall behind her. Her eyes shot open. Bodies flew over her. One caused her crucifix to topple. She landed with a thud, the wind knocked out of her, the sudden s;am of wood against the ground sending a shockwave through her body. As she regained her wits, she managed to catch sight of Aztekoth, apparently unharmed and standing resolutely in place. She was then able to turn to her left and catch sight of that portion of the hall previously hidden to her. Vast flames belched forth, almost reaching as high as the immense timber ceiling. Bodies were strewn about; carnage reigned. Shouts and cries bellowed from every which way.

She couldn't make out just what had happened, though she strongly suspected the identity of this intruder. She had managed to get through to him on her watch distress beacon, prior to being knocked out, after all.

Swiftly, she thought to check her bonds, hoping against hope they had somehow been loosened in the melee. Those hopes paid off. The knot securing her right wrist was no longer as tight as it had been. She now had some leverage to work with. She had to be quick, though. She didn't know how long Aztekoth would remain ignorant of her situation, and she knew not how long Paul could take on Aztekoth's entire army by himself. But knowing Paul as she did, he would have some sort of plan in place.

"Aztekoth!" The Wraith's voice boomed, as if on cue. "Your army of the living dead has been vanquished. Your plans are in disarray, your headquarters compromised again."

Aztekoth took a short step backward, before replying mockingly. "Your overconfidence will be your undoing, Wraith. Nothing you have done will change the destiny of this city. Nothing will alter the course we have taken."

While Leena worked feverishly on freeing her right arm, she caught sight of The Wraith emerging from a plume of black smoke, the Eyes of Judgment on his chest alive in a fierce display of dazzling yellow energy unlike anything she had witnessed before. There was an anger there, a primal rage. She watched him coming toward the stage where she was currently lying and where Aztekoth remained rooted to the spot. Suddenly, two skeletal Aztec warriors jumped him from either side. In an amazing display of ferocious power, The Wraith managed to grab both warriors by the neck in mid-air and smashed their skulls together, pulverizing them instantly. The expression on the Dread Avenger's face, as well as the glowing Eyes of Judgment, gave The Wraith an appearance of avenging death, as though he was the Grim Reaper itself, come to seek savage retribution.

Leena just about had her right arm free, when Aztekoth, perhaps in desperation, leaped forth, and yanked her free from her bonds and up onto her feet. The creature's bony hands touched only the clothed portions of her body, but even so, she could feel their burning touch.

She screamed.

"Hold fast, hero," Aztekoth threatened, "or the life of your female will be forfeit."

The Wraith stopped dead in his tracks, though the anger and determination evident on his face remained. "You are truly desperate to hold a woman hostage thus. You are not worthy to even represent the once glorious Aztec Empire."

"Speak not with such blasphemy, for you will surely perish as all other disbelievers shall."

Aztekoth took a few steps backward, dragging Leena along. The searing heat from Aztekoth's cursed touch was causing her ever-increasing pain. She whimpered in agony, trying hard to check the outward signs of her torment.

"My personal guard will take care of you, Wraith. And then I will have my way with your woman. I will give her a death the likes your worst nightmares could not possibly comprehend."

With that, the creature motioned, and from either side of the stage emerged a handful of well-armed Indians, all outfitted in proper Aztec regalia, all eager to do their master's bidding.

"Farewell, Wraith. I shall think of you occasionally as I sit upon my throne and brush the flies from the carcasses of this city's fallen," Aztekoth said, before laughing so hauntingly as to almost cause Leena to forget the pain in her arms from the creature's touch. She was powerless to stop it dragging her into a rear chamber away from the ensuing carnage, away from the building conflagration and from her beloved Paul. Her final sight of him was as he was readying for battle against at least a half dozen armed warriors. Then the curtained doorway closed and she was in darkness.

* * * * * *

The Dread Avenger clenched his jaw tightly.

Into battle once again.

Seeing his Leena imprisoned had brought his blood to boil. And now, the odds once again stacked against him, that fury had not abated. It would not, not until his love was safe and Aztekoth dealt with. Only then would some sense of inner peace return. But now was not the time for such ruminations. The battle was on, not only with Leena's life at stake, but that of the entire city, perhaps even more.

Three of the Indians charged, spears and shields aloft. The Wraith grabbed the spear of the Indian nearest him and tugged hard, throwing the warrior to the ground, gaining the weapon as a result. Using the spear, he parried the spear thrusts from the other two attacking him. Using their advantage of numbers, they pressed forward, pushing him back without causing any real damage. While defending feverishly, The Wraith noted the third Indian getting to his feet, no doubt eager to rejoin the battle. With the butt end of his spear, The Wraith swiftly smashed it into the crouching warrior's face, removing him as a threat.

Evidently stunned a little by the quick defeat of one of their own, The Wraith took those few seconds to launch a counter-offensive. Spinning his spear around his head, he thrust headlong into the two Indians, parrying, stabbing and blocking with everything he had. He was able to push the two back toward the remaining three warriors, who had held back, no doubt eager to see how well the initial attack would proceed. The Wraith knew full well, though, that such a tactic would not hold long, for the numbers were still against him. He had to even those odds as best he could. Quickly, he ducked under their spear thrusts, and executed a perfect leg sweep, taking the two attacking Indians down. Standing over them, he was able to render both of them unconscious with well placed punches to each of their faces.

The Wraith, thinking quickly, grabbed one of the Indian's shields and added it to his armory. He turned to face his remaining adversaries. The Eyes of Judgment came crackling to life once more, and fear soon became evident on the faces of his enemies.

"You have seen how I have dealt swift justice to your brethren," The Wraith said. "Surrender, or worse will be your fate!"

The three warriors ignored him and issued a guttural cry. They charged him. Using his spear, The Wraith managed to wrench another shield from the arm of his nearest attacker, and smashed it against the head of another. With his own shield, he blocked another thrust and used the opening to send his foot into the warrior's solar plexus, badly winding him. With the Indian bent over, desperately gasping for air, The Wraith came down hard on his head with his shield, cracking the man's skull in the process.

Only one Aztec warrior remained, a particularly burly, muscular specimen. He stood there, menacingly eying the Dread Avenger as though they were facing off in some kind of Wild West duel. The warrior held his spear tightly then started moving it from one hand to the other. In an instant, the warrior hurled the spear with amazing force and accuracy direct for his head. With cat-like reflexes, The Wraith only just managed to raise his shield in time, but such was the power of the throw, the spear penetrated the shield, causing it to shift slightly off course and embed itself into the Dread Avenger's left shoulder.

"Gahhh..." he groaned, pain flaring up and down his arm.

He reached up and wrenched the weapon from his flesh with a grunt. Both the shield and his body armor had offered some measure of protection, but he was still hurt badly. Blood oozed from the wound, coursing a path down his left arm.

The Indian moaned in delight, obviously heartened by his success. He pressed forward, eager to go one further and kill The Wraith. That was his first mistake—over-confidence. The Wraith smiled, for while he was wounded, he was not yet a spent force, and strength and energy still filled his limbs. The Indian was strong, yes, but unarmed and ill-trained in hand-to-hand combat. The warrior attempted blow after blow, but The Wraith dodged, side-stepped them all with relative ease. He executed a powerful scissor-kick, connecting with the warrior's jaw, which sent him sprawling backward, shaky on his feet. The Wraith knew this had to be the moment. He pressed forward, connecting again and again with strong blows to the face and abdomen.

The amount of punishment this Indian could withstand was incredible.

Blow after blow rained down upon the hapless native, yet he remained on his feet, resolute.

Finally, with a wild cry, The Wraith leaped to his feet, and came down hard with a king-hit to the Indian's head, finally sending him to the same fate as his comrades.

Clutching his injured shoulder, which throbbed intensely, The Wraith sprinted for the rear chamber. His beloved Leena's life hung precariously in the balance and he wasn't about to lose her now.

* * * * * *

Leena struggled to free herself from Aztekoth's clutches, but the creature's grip was extremely powerful and each effort to break free was met with powerful resistance. Aztekoth continued to carry her, flailing and kicking, through a darkened corridor or tunnel of some kind. The pain was intolerable. In moments, a weak light began to illuminate their surroundings. They were indeed in some sort of a tunnel, though not one she recognized. Where the creature was taking her she could only dread.

With unconsciousness—perhaps even death—beckoning, the creature came to a stop and dropped her. They were now in what appeared to be some kind of rudimentary bedchamber, extremely filthy, and the air was thick with dust and with the stench of death Leena had smelt too often as of late. Aztekoth turned his back to her, moving over to what she thought served as his bed, which was nothing more than a pile of rotting rags and soiled wool.

She sat there, injured and in pain, though able to catch her breath and regain some measure of strength. She was grateful that her suit took at least some of the brunt of Aztekoth's burning touch. Skintight as it was, it was made of a flame retardant polymer of Max's design and thus proved more protective than its appearance would otherwise indicate.

If she was going to do anything, now was the time.

She lunged at the creature, jumping up onto his back, and gripped his hooded head tightly. Aztekoth swiveled around, with Leena still hanging on for dear life. She tore the hood from his head.

She screamed.

~ Chapter 17 ~

Leena fell to the hard, dust strewn ground with a thud. She looked up at Aztekoth. Melted flesh somehow still sat on the creature's skull, the bone of which was partially visible. The flesh appeared fetid, rancid and smelled awful. Maggots crawled over the putrid mess that was his face. There were no eyes, only hollow sockets displaying glowing red slits deep within. With such an appearance, it was hard to describe the creature as alive or even human.

She felt a strong urge to throw up.

"You are sickened?" the creature finally spoke as he pulled the hood back over his head. "No matter. For as soon as I have the Cortes Stone within my grasp and incant the sacred words, I shall be whole once again."

"Sinner!" came a familiar voice. "Your plans for this city have been torn asunder. Now you must pay the ultimate price!"

"You!" Aztekoth shrieked, clearly shocked. "How you continually manage to survive—"

"You are all that is left," The Wraith boomed, the Eyes of Judgment on his chest coming to life. "Your plans have been destroyed, your race forced back into extinction. Now there is only you. And me!"

Leena saw her beloved's shoulder wound, which was bleeding more freely than she would have liked, but the look of intensity on his face, the power and strength in his voice proved to her that his wound was the last thing on his mind. In fact, despite Aztekoth's seeming invincibility to this point, it was The Wraith who now had the ascendancy, who now appeared all-powerful.

"You consider yourself my equal? My superior?" Aztekoth mocked. "You are a gnat. A bug I will squash under foot as I intend this entire city!"

Furious, the creature ignored Leena and lunged at The Wraith, intent on wreaking vengeance against the man who had put a halt to his far-reaching plans of horror and conquest. Leena stood, eager to help as best she might in what could well be the last foe she or The Wraith would ever face.

* * * * * *

For a creature of such immense size, Aztekoth moved with amazing speed. The Wraith could do nothing to evade his headlong thrust and took the brunt of the creature's force head on. The two combatants hit the floor with a thud, knocking the wind from the Dread Avenger. They rolled around, wrestling. The Wraith knew deep down this would be it. Either he or his adversary would fall here and the fate of the city lay in the hands of the victor.

The creature was on his feet in an instant, displaying an agility that surprised The Wraith. Aztekoth yanked him to his feet in the blink of an eye. The creature, enraged, his red eyes glowing fiercely, squeezed the Dread Avenger by the throat and lifted him clear off the ground with the one arm.

"Now you will feel the true power of Aztekoth. You will *burn* as you deserve!"

The Wraith struggled to free himself, but Aztekoth's strength was overwhelming. Despite his high collar protecting him from the brunt of the force being exerted, The Wraith started to feel the searing heat penetrate to his skin, as well as the strong grip of Aztekoth's bony fingers. He flailed about with his legs, tried to break the creature's grip, but nothing seemed to work. With blackness looming, creeping in at the edges of his vision, The Wraith could do nothing. He was in the creature's thrall, totally and utterly.

My darling Leena...

Suddenly, he was free, having been dropped to the floor. The Wraith fell on his knees, hacked the air back into his lungs. Leena stood there holding a rotten piece of wood. It took him a few moments to realize what occurred. Aztekoth put a hand to his head then violently swatted Leena down with a backward slap, sending her sprawling.

It was now or never. Angered beyond measure, The Wraith took this opportunity.

He jumped onto Aztekoth, catching him completely unaware, and took him to the floor. He managed to quickly pin the creature down and allowed the Eyes of Judgment to once again burst to life.

"Stare into the flames of your guilt," The Wraith barked. "Allow your soul to be consumed within it. The pain and horror you have inflicted upon others will now bathe you in its gloom."

The Wraith's Judgment Stare began to take hold before the creature could break free from his grasp. The intense energies from the Eyes enveloped Aztekoth, bathing him in a liquid-like energy, surrounding the creature in his entirety. The look upon Aztekoth's face, within his very eyes—such a look of horror, an expression of fear and revulsion The Wraith had never witnessed before, not even from the Cobra or Magnus Khan. Aztekoth screamed and started to thrash violently. The Wraith tried to hang on, for the Eyes of Judgment were not yet done delivering their verdict.

Still screaming, Aztekoth threw The Wraith from him, lurched to his feet, and staggered further into the labyrinthine underground den, disappearing down a darkened tunnel. The Wraith couldn't let him escape again. He doubted whether the Judgment Stare had been totally successful, though it was clear some measure of effect had been achieved. Before following, he quickly checked on Leena. She had a cut along her right temple, no doubt from the creature's sharp bony knuckles, and her torso was pockmarked with burn marks, but she appeared otherwise unharmed albeit unconscious. The Dread Avenger promptly tended to her wounds, and once finished, eyed the blackness of the tunnel behind him through narrow slits. This could be a trap, but I dare not allow Aztekoth to escape. Too much is still at stake to risk it.

There was nothing else for it. Time was of the essence. Though it pained him to do so, he left Leena behind and plunged headlong down the pitch black tunnel in pursuit of his prey.

Instinctively, the Dread Avenger reached up to his left temple, activating the infra-red lenses in his cowl. The narrow, cobblestoned path appeared before him snaking this way and that. He stopped for a moment, his panting somewhat obscuring his attempt to detect the creature's fleeing footfalls. He held his breath to silence himself.

Barely, he could just make out a distinctive clip-clop of the creature's bony feet coming down on the hard surface of the tunnel. The Wraith continued his pursuit and poured on the speed.

Suddenly, despite the darkness, he was filled with a sense he'd been in this section of the den before. Almost as suddenly, he entered into a deep grotto with very high ceilings before emerging onto a large viaduct with an immense body of water spilling out underneath. And there, at the far end of the familiar causeway, stood Aztekoth!

"You pursue me to your grave," Aztekoth boomed, apparently having recovered from his ordeal at the hands of the Eyes of Judgment.

"You are now weaker," The Wraith fired back, trying to be heard over the cacophony from the torrent of water beneath them. "The Eyes of Judgment have affected you, affected your very soul. You are now truly alone."

"You are a fool, Wraith. I will end this once and for all here. Your beloved city, everything you hold dear, will pay the price of your defiance."

"You are right," he replied. "It ends here."

Aztekoth jumped and dove through the air, arms outstretched, eyes aglow. This time, The Wraith was prepared. He produced his grapnel gun and fired it into the ceiling high above before Aztekoth reached him, pulling himself up and out of harm's way. Infuriated, the creature could do nothing but look on. Then, in a split-second, The Wraith pressed a button on the grapnel's handle and dropped at breakneck speed back down toward his adversary. Before Aztekoth knew what hit him, The Wraith lashed out with a powerful kick to the head, sending the creature to the ground, hard.

The Wraith regained his footing atop the narrow brick viaduct. Aztekoth was weakened. A blow such as that, while powerful enough to take out most enemies, would have been close to useless against the creature earlier. He had been right: the Eyes of Judgment had inflicted some measure of damage upon him. Just how much was the question.

Before The Wraith could take advantage of Aztekoth's apparent weakness, the creature stood and faced the Dread Avenger once again. Without another word being spoken, Aztekoth charged. The Wraith knew that even with the creature potentially weakened, he could not match him for strength let alone win fighting him toe-to-toe. So, with Aztekoth practically upon him, he brought forth the Eyes of Judgment once more, stopping the creature in his tracks.

"Cease battling the inevitable. You have lost. Your cause is at an end. Your war with humanity is no more," The Wraith said.

Aztekoth staggered back, fear evident in his red eyes. The creature stumbled, struggling to keep his footing as The Wraith pressed forward, the Eyes of Judgment crackling bright and fierce, driving him backward. In desperation, Aztekoth lunged forward, grabbed the Dread Avenger by the throat and attempted to regain the offensive, to choke the life from his enemy. His bony fingers still had immense strength, not to mention his burning touch, and The Wraith fought hard to break the creature's hold. Even weakened, even affected by the Judgment Stare now being exerted once again upon him, Aztekoth was still a most powerful opponent.

"You have not won yet. The war is never over," Aztekoth spat with fury.

At that moment, The Wraith's Eyes of Judgment sparked to life in even greater bouts of energy and light. Aztekoth's face was bathed in the luminous, yellow energy, almost electrical. Lightning bolts coursed over and through Aztekoth in such a dazzling display that The Wraith wondered if anything was wrong. The Eyes of Judgment hadn't acted in this way since his battle with Magnus Khan, and this surpassed that powerful display. He'd never known the Eyes to be so powerful, so attuned to the mortal dangers posed to his person, so attuned to the evil he was now battling. As he watched Aztekoth stumble and writhe backward, the creature whimpering in agony, he wondered just what other secrets his powers might yield in the future.

"What have you done to me?" Aztekoth managed to utter. "What manner of being are you?"

He continued to squirm in great difficulty, the energies still flowing around him—through him—even though he was now some distance away. In seconds, he reached the edge of the viaduct, but he had lost total control of his movement. He was now in the complete thrall of the energy emitted by the Eyes of Judgment. The Wraith could do nothing but watch. In the split second he had left, Aztekoth looked up, stared at The Wraith with helpless eyes . . . and toppled backward. The Wraith rushed to the edge, peered over into the chasm, but all there was a dreadful cauldron of swirling water and seething foam.

Aztekoth's body was nowhere to be found.

* * * * * *

Both Max and Leena moved to The Wraith's side at the edge of the treacherous viaduct. Leena didn't know how long her love had stood there, peering over the side, but she took his arm, glad to have him safe and with her once again.

The three stood there quietly for some time before Max broke the silence. "It's over. We've won."

The Wraith turned to face his friend. "I'll believe that when we find the body. Until then, I remain on alert."

With that, he stalked off, leaving both Leena and Max behind. Leena looked to the Irishman. They both knew The Wraith was right, but she hoped against hope the struggle was at an end, that Aztekoth was dead and buried along with his plans for conquest and destruction.

She and Max turned from the edge of the viaduct and made their way to follow The Wraith and return home.

~ Chapter 18 ~

Robert Latham put the phone back in its cradle, then proceeded to pace from one side of his palatial office to the other. Metro City—*his* city—had once again become a battlefield for every nut and egomaniac that chose it to stake their claim on the world. And once again, they had proven a major headache in his plans for the city. Just now he received word of The Wraith's triumph over this latest pest, Aztekoth, whom he had thought he vanquished earlier. Latham smiled, realizing the irony of the situation. Here, for the first time, he was happy The Wraith had proven victorious. Not only had that blasted Dread Avenger of the Underworld brought the city back into the crime lord's control, but he remained alive, now long enough for Latham to finally kill him, as he'd often dreamed of doing.

"Mr. Latham, are you sure you want to go through with this? At least leave the stone under lock and key at the Gallery," Grieco said, having just appeared at the office door.

Latham shot him an angry look. "Of course, or I would not have authorized as much," he said. "This parade must go on, complete with the Cortes Stone. I've just spoken with the mayor and assured him of this fact. We have to show the world this city's spirit cannot be trodden on by interlopers. We have to show everyone hope cannot be extinguished."

Grieco smiled at his boss. "You sound like one of those hero types."

Latham failed to appreciate the comparison. He frowned sternly at his deputy and said nothing.

"I'll make all the arrangements, then," Grieco finally said, still grinning ever-so-slightly. He quickly retreated from the office.

Latham took a seat at his plush brown, Spanish leather chair, pulled an expensive—and illegal—Cuban cigar from its ornate silver case at the head of his desk, removed the band, snipped the tip and lit it. Leaning back, he blew smoke rings and began to relax. Somewhat.

Yes, the city is back under my control, and what better way to fully exemplify that fact than to push forward with the parade and show everyone—especially The Wraith—that I am still here and still in control. He smiled. Yes, that made him feel better. Much better.

* * * * * *

Paul Sanderson sat pensively in his antique brown leather wing chair in the Sanderson House study library, the favorite part of his expansive home. Surrounded by his books, by the furnishings of the Victorian era he favored, he felt more at home here than practically anywhere else. Perhaps even more so than the Lair. However, today his mind was on more important things. He couldn't shake the feeling that perhaps this wasn't over yet. They had, as yet, not recovered Aztekoth's body and that worried him. He knew if the monster had truly been vanquished, the seething water could very well have carried the body out into the vastness of the ocean. Even so, Paul could not help but be concerned. A creature as powerful and as immersed in the supernatural as Aztekoth was...anything could be possible. Was he even truly alive to begin with? And therefore, did the rules of life and death even apply to such a creature? It was a puzzle with no answer.

Leena appeared with two cups of tea. She placed one on the little table at his side, while she held the other in her hand as she took a seat in the chair nearest him.

"Thanks, darling," Paul said warmly as he took a sip of his favorite blend, Earl Grey. "Mmmm, just right."

"Simpson's trained me in the arcane ways of brewing tea," she said with a smile. "There's a lot more to it than I originally thought."

He smiled wanly but couldn't shake his mood of impending dread, that perhaps Aztekoth was still alive, still planning his next move and still able to make good on his many threats. He then realized he was staring at the carpet, frowning. He looked up to face his beloved. The concern on her face was clearly evident.

"I'm sorry, darling. I just can't help feel we haven't seen the last of Aztekoth. And that worries me. Have we heard back from Max yet with the latest?"

"Not yet, though I doubt there's any news to report. With the sewers so swollen with the recent downpours, there's no hope of finding a body amongst that raging inferno," she said.

"You're right. I know you're right. But until or unless we find Aztekoth's remains, I won't rest easy. We're dealing with too powerful an enemy to become complacent. We almost lost this city, almost lost everything."

She moved over to him, knelt down in front of him and took his hands. "I know, darling. We're doing everything we can. We'll know more soon, I'm sure."

Paul took her hands in his and smiled lovingly at her. The wound on her right temple reminded him of the ordeal the night before. She had needed six stitches, which hurt him almost as much as it had her. His shoulder was sore, too, but he knew it would heal well.

He gazed into her beautiful blue eyes. She always knew the right things to say and knew always how to make him feel better. He kissed her right hand. "Thank you, love. I hope so. I really do."

* * * * * *

Bob Sloan lurched through the workroom toward his messy desk. It was early morning, and while the immediate threat of Aztekoth appeared to have dissipated, the work of a Metro City police detective was never-ending, and this day was no exception. Despite it being early, Sloan was somewhat surprised to find Perez seated by the edge of his desk.

"You're an early riser," he said. "Nothing better to do than come to work?"

"I could say the same for you, Bob. What does your wife have to say about this?"

"Oh, you know, happy to get me out of the house."

"Yeah, right," Perez said. She changed the subject. "Word's just come in that the mayor and Robert Latham have agreed to move forward with the street parade, including the Cortes Stone. Can you believe that? We're still counting our dead and these politicians want to celebrate!"

"Sounds like pure Latham to me," he said. "When's this supposed to take place?"

"Tomorrow, as originally scheduled."

Sloan groaned a little. "They could have at least delayed it a little. How is the city supposed to be able to clean itself up by tomorrow?"

"I don't know. I just don't know."

Sloan eyed her carefully. Her eyes looked glassy, as though she was about to cry and didn't look at all herself. The strong, forthright lady he knew her to be suddenly looked like a mere shadow of her former self. He sat down in his chair. Perez was always the positive one, always the one who saw the glass as half full, always the one to lift him out of the morass he found himself in emotionally. But now.... Then he remembered the black mood he had found himself in only recently. That mood had instantly vanished as soon as he'd had his dream. Or had it been a vision?

"Perez, is anything wrong?" he enquired.

She looked at him with soulful eyes, appearing almost as if tears were about to flow there and then. "I don't know, Bob. I feel a weight on my heart that I can't explain. Maybe the job is getting to me more than I thought. Maybe it's this latest Aztekoth business." She took a deep breath. "I honestly don't know."

Those words rung true with him. They were the very words he had used himself just a few short days ago. He, too, had this feeling of hopelessness, of a blackening of his soul that had come from nowhere but still somehow felt as if it had festered for some time. No matter where it came from, he'd found it nigh on debilitating. And, as suddenly as it had appeared, it vanished after he had his...he didn't know what he had experienced. All he knew was he had been blessed with a truth that had cleansed him somehow. It wasn't something he could put into words and it certainly wasn't something he could tell a soul about. But he knew it to be the truth and that was enough.

"Perez, I don't know what to say. Maybe you should speak with the precinct counselor? Heck, you can talk to me anytime."

He felt helpless. He knew of nothing else he could suggest that could help her. Perhaps her talking it over with a professional would be of some assistance to her. Even talking to him might help—though he knew there was only so much he could do or say—but he knew he could be a good listener.

"Maybe I should. Yeah, maybe. We'll see," she said finally, before standing and moving over to her own desk and sitting down.

Sloan eyed her with concern. He looked around at the others who had already reported early for work and those who were about to knock off for the day. He expected them all to look tired, somewhat bedraggled after the events of the last few days. But even so, the expressions on all their faces were something else. Something more. Alarm bells rang inside him. He could tell they were afflicted with the same blackness of mood he had earlier, and which was now affecting Perez. What was going on here? And just how many were afflicted? He had no answers, but he intended on finding them. And quickly.

* * * * * *

As the early morning sun crept over the imposing Metro City skyline on Saturday, The Wraith sat hunched atop the Latham Towers complex, the city's highest building. Today was the day of the anniversary street parade, and with Latham insisting it go ahead—with the Cortes Stone front and center no less—he knew that if Aztekoth was still alive, if he was still able to make some form of attack, it would be here during this parade.

The Wraith would be ready.

On the street below, he could make out the organizers readying some of the many intricate floats. There were floats with a plethora of small, colorful balloons, floats featuring much larger balloons with all manner of cartoon and other characters in literature, such as Felix the Cat, Garfield, Snow White and other Disney cartoon characters and Sherlock Holmes, among many others. All the floats featured the central character displayed high above, while on the float's surface were flowers and people dressed in character. And, to his shock, there was even a float with a massive balloon featuring himself, The Wraith, or at least that's what he thought it looked like. It bore little resemblance to how he really looked, though. Each float was trucked into position and further dressed to make it just right for the start of the parade, which was still some time off.

"Darling, are you there?" Leena's voice came over his in-cowl communication system.

"Yes, Leena. Any sign of Aztekoth?"

"None, although if he was to make an appearance, it might be a little early. There's been no sign of the Cortes Stone yet."

"Understood. Keep in touch," he said, and signed off.

He then checked in with Max and received the same negative result. As frustrating as it was, he realized it *was* most likely too early for any potential result. Still, he had a gut feeling Aztekoth *was* still alive and that the creature *would* make an appearance, a last ditch gambit at salvation and ultimate victory. And it was his job to stop that, no matter the cost.

As the morning stretched on, The Wraith kept a close watch on the parade, while also using his mini-binoculars to search as much throughout the city as his current vantage point allowed. At regular intervals, Max and Leena reported their findings. As the minutes dragged into hours, the parade now progressing, there was still no sign of Aztekoth.

Could I have been wrong? Could the monster truly have perished in the sewers below?

His gut continued to say otherwise, so he and his team carried on, watching, waiting.

The parade was now on in full force, with the floats and exhibits streaming down Metro's main thoroughfare. Despite what the city had gone through only a few days before, the public had come out in high numbers, which worried the Dread Avenger even more. If Aztekoth was to strike, the potential for civilian casualties would be high. That was unacceptable. Still, there had been no sign of an Aztec float, no sign of the Cortes Stone—the fake Cortes Stone that is, as The Wraith had thought it best to wait a little more before returning the real stone, which was still safely tucked away in his Lair. If Aztekoth was to reappear, the creature would not gain his most valued prize.

The procession of complex and beautiful floats continued to flow down the street. Finally, as the end came into view, The Wraith spotted the float that he'd been waiting for. It was rather garishly outfitted in Aztec decorations and other paraphernalia, including pottery, carvings, weaponry and jewelry. And there, at the rear, inside a Perspex case, was the replica stone, surrounded by two burly and armed guards. As it brought up the rear of the lengthy and popular event, The Wraith watched on through ever-narrowing eyes. The police were out in force, protecting the important civic event as well as keeping the crowd at bay. Even so, if Aztekoth was to appear, he doubted they would be enough to stop him.

As if in reply to that thought, the creature suddenly appeared by the float's side, jumped aboard it, brutally smashed one of the onboard guards down, while grabbing the other by the arm, disintegrating the poor fellow in seconds.

Oh no, The Wraith thought.

Not wasting another second, he leaped over the threshold, parachuted down to the ground using his cape to slow his descent, always keeping a stern eye on the activities of his mortal enemy below.

Before the police could properly react, Aztekoth reached for the Perspex case, smashed it open and raised his arms to the heavens.

"At last, salvation is mine," Aztekoth cried.

The Wraith raced toward the Aztec float, eager to do whatever it took to stop this evil creature. Aztekoth reached down to the Cortes Stone, lifted it from its base and gazed at it intently. The creature held it high above his head then seemed to have caught sight of The Wraith sprinting toward him.

"You are too late, Wraith," he wailed. "Salvation is mine, and with it the unlimited power of the elders."

The Wraith pressed forward, just about there, but he was too late—Aztekoth was too quick. The creature began reciting a series of unintelligible incantations. In moments, it was over, and the creature shrieked with delight. Victory was his!

"It's over. I have won! Watch now as I am reborn, and let this city and its people tremble at the supreme power of Aztekoth!"

Aztekoth stood there, his body quivering with strength and ecstasy. Time stopped; The Wraith, fearing that despite the true stone having been replaced with a forgery, it had been all for naught. The Wraith leaped aboard the float and readied himself for battle. Aztekoth clenched his bony fists together, flexing his joints. And then, when all appeared hopeless, Aztekoth screamed.

"No, this can't be happening. Salvation was finally mine. The power was mine!"

The Wraith could do nothing but look on in horror, for Aztekoth's body began to shudder then sway slightly before breaking out into violent fits, as though the creature was suffering from a vicious form of epilepsy. Aztekoth shrieked in abject torment, bent forward, held his arms out toward The Wraith as though asking—begging—for forgiveness. Then it was over. With one last moan of anguish, Aztekoth's body crumbled to dust, leaving only his tattered rags as testament to his existence.

The Wraith blinked his eyes for a few moments. Was the creature truly destroyed? Was the nightmare the city had endured finally at an end? He could scarcely believe it, and yet, he knew it to be true: the nightmare *was* over. He allowed himself a further moment to breathe more easily, but only a moment, for he realized the eyes of the hundreds—*thousands* —of onlookers were trained solely on him, and, to make matters worse, it was now the middle of the day. The sun, though bright, was hidden behind clouds. The crowd was silent, staring at the Dread Avenger as though they were deer caught in the headlights of an oncoming vehicle. The Wraith dared not tarry a moment longer. He produced his grapnel gun from his belt, aimed it skyward and fired. Attached safely to a building ledge high above, he pressed the retract button on the handle, and shot upwards at high-speed. A few moments more, and he was gone, up and over the roof and out of sight of the crowd below.

~ Epilogue ~

Paul woke with a start. He checked the bedside clock. It was just before midnight. Usually at this time of night, he was out on patrol, but Leena had convinced him to take a night off from work. Their recent battles with Aztekoth had left them both wounded, and all were drained, both physically and mentally, so he had reluctantly agreed to her request. Even so, it was hard for him to let go of such long-held traditions, and sleep was even harder to come by as a result.

"Hmmm? You okay, darling?" Leena said, half-muzzy with sleep.

"It's okay, honey. Go back to sleep."

Leena stirred herself. "Paul, what is it? I know you. I can tell when something's bothering you." She sat up to face him and turned on the bedside lamp.

"When the people spotted me," he said reluctantly, "stared right at me, I couldn't help but notice something. A feeling. A sense . . ." It was difficult to find the words to describe just how it felt.

"What do you mean, 'a feeling'? Coming from the people?"

"It's hard to describe, but...yes, I think so."

"What kind of feeling?"

Paul looked at her. "Of anger. No. Hatred."

Leena stared at him with confusion in her eyes, but said nothing in reply. No words needed to be said in that moment. Paul took her in his arms, doing their best to make the rest of the world's troubles disappear, if only for a moment. They were lost in their love and their devotion for each other.

Nothing else mattered.

* * * * * *

The following few days had been warm and dry, with the long non-existent sun having returned in all its glory, brightening up what had been a dreary few weeks and helping to burn away the excess water that still filled the city streets. But now that night had fallen, the city had once again taken on its sinister form, with long, dark shadows striking forth here and there, moving about as though the city was a haven for ghosts and demons. With what the city had been through as of late, Sloan began to wonder if that description was perhaps more accurate than he ever dared think.

"I hear you've been looking for me," The Wraith said, appearing from nowhere atop the police headquarters building at the furthest edge away from Sloan.

"Jeez, don't do that," Sloan said, slightly embarrassed to be showing such emotion. He prided himself on his strength and fortitude. "How'd you know I'd be up here now?"

"What do you want, Sloan? You've been leaving messages all over town for days with every lowlife and scum, letting them know you wanted to see me."

Sloan stepped forward slowly, not wanting to scare the masked man off. The Dread Avenger remained rooted to the spot, somehow merging with the darkness that surrounded them both.

"I didn't know how else to contact you. It's not as though we have some signal to call you when we need you," Sloan said. The Wraith remained still and silent. "I just wanted you to know that I'm okay with you being in this town. I'm okay with everything."

"I wasn't aware I required your permission to be here," The Wraith said pointedly.

Sloan stopped mid stride. Opening up like this wasn't his strong suit. Not by a long shot, but he had to at least try to clear the air without giving too much away.

"That's not what I meant," he said.

The Wraith shifted his weight ever-so-slightly, taking on a somewhat less commanding pose. "Why the change of heart?"

Sloan smiled weakly. "Let's just say I know where you're coming from. And...I now know I can trust you."

Sloan wasn't sure, but he could have sworn he saw The Wraith smile for a split-second, but then it was gone as quickly as it had appeared. The Dread Avenger turned around as if to leave and for a moment, he thought the man would disappear, back into the ether of another murky Metro night. But The Wraith stopped, turned back and took a step forward. A powerful arm shot outward, and Sloan took it without having to think. They shook, establishing a bond he knew would never be broken.

Strong grip, Sloan thought, and he smiled.

And with that, The Wraith took a step backward, off the roof and into the night.

~ Author's Note ~

This is the book I'm proudest to re-present to you, my dear readers. You see, I was very disappointed with the original version of this book, which was first published in 2009 (too long after it had been finished for my tastes). No offense to the previous editor/publisher, but it *was* poorly edited and formatted, which greatly displeased me. Now, finally, I can present this book as I've always wanted it to be presented and you can take advantage of this great story anew. I hope you enjoyed it.

As always, I need to thank a few people, which I will proceed to do now. To my wife goes the greatest thanks. Jennifer is always there for me, loving and caring for me, and her literary advice is always welcome. To my family, thank you for always being there for me also. To my Trinity

Comics team—Jeff Welborn, Roland Bird, Joel Danford, Jeff Austin, Adam O. Pruett, Rick Hannah and Splash!, thanks for always making me look better than I actually am.

Following this is a sneak peek at the next book in *The Wraith Adventures* series, *Cry of the Werewolf* (my personal favorite). Please read further and perhaps, if you so choose, check out some of the other books in the series. Details of those are located on the following pages.

Thank you.

Frank Dirscherl
Wollongong NSW, 2013

CRY OF THE WEREWOLF
~ Sneak peek ~

Here is a special sneak peek at the following novel in the series, *Cry of the Werewolf.* Please enjoy chapter 1 of this exciting book...

~ Chapter 1 ~

Thump. Thump. Thump. Eddie's heart was beating in his chest like a hammer. He gulped, forcing the build-up of bile back down his throat. He looked down at his hands—they were shaking as though he was an old man. He hated that, hated how Nick had been able to talk him into this. Nick was able to talk him into anything, and Eddie cursed under his breath the weakness he had shown, had always shown.

Now he found himself here, in this revolting back alley which stank of rotting fish and human waste. Earlier that night, Nick had spotted a well-to-do looking family—husband, wife and a young boy—wandering through the city, clearly lost, but unwilling to ask for help. Asking for help could be suicidal in a city like Metro and so they were unable to get their bearings. They obviously weren't locals.

Nick had marked them and he and Eddie had followed their course from the better part of the city to their current position in the seedier section. It was Nick's idea to waylay them as soon as he thought it best to do so. He then left to find the perfect position of attack while he ordered Eddie to keep watch on them, and anyone else who may get too close. So, Eddie did what he was told; he watched and he waited.

He saw no sign of Nick, but the family was there, wandering helplessly toward their doom. There were few people about, certainly nobody interested in the potential rich pickings Nick had identified. Eddie watched closely as the family turned into a small side-alley around the corner from his current vantage point. Then he heard the scream.

He ran round the corner and sprinted for the alley the family had drifted into. Rounding the corner he saw the man lying on the filthy ground in a pool of blood. His wife and boy were huddled nearby and the woman was yelping loudly. Nick was standing there, pointing his gun at them, before noticing Eddie.

"Run, you idiot. Run!" Nick barked.

Eddie did so, turning and sprinting as best he could. Nick easily passed him an instant later. Eddie ran as fast as he could, trying to keep pace with Nick. His heart was beating so furiously he thought it would burst free from his chest, such was the intensity of his emotions. They rounded several more corners, weaving their way through the maze of seedy back alleys and side-streets for which Metro City was infamous.

In the haze of their excitement, Eddie suddenly realized where they were going. He knew this part of town; he and Nick hung out there quite regularly. Soon he spotted the building he'd suspected Nick was heading for and the urine stained timber door at its rear. Not wasting a second to catch their breaths, Nick barged through the door, with Eddie close at his heels, up the dimly lit stairs and out onto the roof.

Settling behind a large, bulbous smoke stack, Nick plopped down onto a soiled, tattered blanket. Eddie sat down next to him, his feet extending out onto the gravel.

"Our number came up today, Eddie-boy," Nick said, as he rifled through what must have been the man's wallet. It was stuffed full of cash and cards. Nick's face lit up with each new find. "Hey, American Express card...don't leave home without it." He laughed.

"What happened back there?" Eddie asked, still breathless from what had just occurred.

"I took what was rightfully ours," Nick said, snorting. "That guy's clearly loaded. He can afford to give some of it over to charity." He laughed again.

"But, he was bleeding. He might be—"

"Look," Nick interrupted, "I gave him a crack on the skull. Who cares? A guy like that has insurance." He now had the cash out in both hands, vaguely counting the bills.

"With yer...yer gun?" Eddie stammered. He felt the sweat beading on his brow. Stealing was one thing, and he hated even that, but murder? That was a whole new kettle of fish, one he wanted no part of. And yet...

"Yeah, with my gun," Nick spat. "It was all I had. He was lucky I didn't plug him with it. Now shut up, will ya? I'm trying to count."

"You shouldna' turned the gun on that kid, man," Eddie said, ignoring Nick. He was scared, and when he was scared, he blathered. "You shouldna' turned the gun on that kid."

"You want your cut of this money or not?" Nick said, annoyed. "Now shut the hell up!"

Eddie complied. He was scared of the whole situation, but he was more scared of Nick right there and then. He leaned back against the smoke stack, sullen. In that moment, he hated himself, hated the city, hated the life in which he was born into. He'd never had much of anything in life, that was true, but of late he'd felt more depressed and hatred toward anything and everything than ever before. And he didn't know why. He looked down at his hands again. They were still shaking.

Damn Nick, damn everything.

"What was that?" Eddie whispered suddenly.

"Wha—?" Nick replied vacantly.

"Didn't you just hear that? Sounded like footsteps, up here on the rooftop."

"Shut up, I din't hear anythin'."

Then came the noise again, louder. Closer. Footsteps on gravel.

"Crap, I heard that," Nick said, jumping to his feet.

Eddie followed suit. They both turned at the same instant, taking a few steps back. There, up on the smoke stack itself, was an unholy apparition. The black shape had a leathery cape that was outstretched ominously and monstrous eyes on its chest that glowed an appalling yellow. A fierce energy crackled around and from within it.

Eddie wanted to scream. He opened his mouth but nothing came out. Nick just stood there, aghast at the sight before them.

"You who have caused pain to others," the apparition moaned in a terrifyingly deep, rasping voice, "now is your time of judgment." The shape dropped down onto the gravel before them with such an ease and grace as to be not human. Before Nick could react, a powerful leg snaked out, catching him fully in the midriff, winding him badly. He dropped to his knees in great pain. An instant later, a powerful fist sent Nick into a deep slumber. He never knew what hit him.

Eddie knew he had to get away, had to escape this monster before him. He turned quickly and ran.

The access door, must reach the access door. Once I'm in there, I can drop down the stairs and be out in the alley. I can blend in with the darkness and escape easily.

Before he was able to move more than a few feet, something entangled around his ankles. And he fell, his face smashing harshly onto the gravel floor. Eddie cried out in pain and anguish, struggled and tried to break free. But he was pulled backward, back toward the monster. He clawed desperately, trying to gain some sort of handhold, but all he got was handfuls of dirt and gravel. He kept at it, rubbing his fingers raw, the blood starting to flow. But there was no escape. The monster had him.

In the instant that followed, Eddie had time only to roll around, for the second he did so, the monster had its massive hands on his collar, yanking him up, clean off the ground as though he was a rag doll. Eddie panicked, flailed his legs about in abject terror.

"What are you?" he shrieked.

The monster was now in Eddie's face, the eyes on its chest still crackling with intense electrical energy. Despite his fear, despite everything, he could now make out who his attacker was, the identity of the monster who had him in his thrall—it was The Wraith!

"I am your worst nightmare," The Wraith growled. "I am your conscience. Let your soul be cleansed by the Eyes of Judgment. Let your soul be burned with the guilt of your lifetime of sin!"

The Dread Avenger dropped Eddie but did not release him. He grabbed him by his head and forced him to peer down into the Eyes.

Eddie screamed.

* * * * * *

A nearby fog horn blared. A thick, murky fog was starting to make its way ashore, drifting in slowly but surely from the Atlantic. Steve glanced up at the milky build-up in the sky now beginning to envelop him and lit a cigarette. Soon he would be able to see very little, save the powerful spotlight that stood firmly above him sending slivers of light through the gloom. The sound of waves slapping intensely against the pylons of the nearby wharf proved somewhat comforting to Steve. It was a sound he was well familiar with.

He waited and watched as best he could. Tonight would be the night he became a big man in Charlie Grieco's new empire. He smirked at the thought of it and drew again from his self-rolled cigarette. Grieco had been planning to topple his boss Robert Latham for years. Now, apparently, that time had come. Grieco had promised him a prime position in the new organization, and he'd taken him up on the offer wholeheartedly. No longer would he be a mere delivery boy for the city's scum. No longer would he put his very life on the line on an almost daily basis for next to nothing. No, he was destined for bigger things. Tonight was the night.

Through the din, he could make out the noise of a tug approaching the wharf.

This must be it, he thought.

With his cigarette clamped tightly between his thin lips, Steve made his way forward. Droplets of water from the fog beaded his brow and he pulled the collar of his woolen overcoat up over his neck. As he trudged down the rickety steps toward the wharf, he squinted, trying to peer through the murk. By this time the fog had thickened, but he could still see his own hand in front of his face. He continued walking toward the noise of the incoming tug.

"Steve. That you?" a voice Steve thought familiar cried out.

"Yeah," he replied, somewhat cautious.

Fast approaching footsteps could be heard and Steve stopped. He braced himself. In seconds, the shape of a man could be vaguely seen. It was Charlie Grieco.

"Good to see you here, Steve," Grieco said, smiling as he did so. "This shipment's gonna' make me, big time. And you too."

"Great, great," Steve said back. "But what exactly are you bringing in tonight? And I didn't know you'd be here yourself. I thought I'd be taking charge of delivery."

Grieco smiled again. "Steve...my whole future depends upon this shipment. Yours too. I couldn't let anything go wrong, not with something so important," he said confidently.

Grieco put his arm over Steve's shoulder, and they made their way along the wharf toward the shore.

"Don't worry, I'll let you handle everything, as promised. I'll just stand to one side and supervise. It's nice to know my future is in good hands," Grieco said.

Steve stopped short and faced Grieco. Back under the spotlight where he'd previously stood, Grieco's features were a little clearer to make out in the extreme weather conditions.

"But, what are we bringing in here?" he asked again.

"Weapons, drugs, you name it. Everything we need, without Latham's knowledge. This is it, I tell you. This is it."

Without sound or warning and seemingly from nowhere, a huge shape dropped down between them. In an instant, Grieco was down and the shape loomed before Steve like some hideous creature from the depths of hell. Strobing yellow energy—*are they eyes?*—blazed on the shape's chest. Steve made to move, but couldn't. He was rooted to the spot.

"This city is not yours to poison with your filth," the shape growled.

Steve managed to stagger backward slightly. It was then that he realized who his antagonist was. The Wraith.

"I...I..." Steve managed to stutter.

"You will know what pain and misery you have caused others. Your soul will be purged of its evil."

Even in the ever-thickening fog, Steve could just make out Charlie Grieco sneaking up behind The Wraith. Grieco took a swing at the Dread Avenger's head, but The Wraith ducked swiftly as though he had eyes in the back of his head. The Wraith lashed out with a backhand punch, catching Grieco square on the chin, knocking him down once again.

"No, not like this. Not when everything was within my grasp," Grieco shrieked as he rubbed some blood from his lips.

The Wraith grabbed Steve and sent him in a heap beside his boss.

"Your time of power within the city is at an end," The Wraith growled. "And Robert Latham is next."

Realization crossed Grieco's face, Steve noticed.

"Latham? No...could it have been? He found me out?" He paused for thought. "That...that...he ratted me out. To his greatest enemy, he ratted me out."

With one hand on each of their collars, The Wraith yanked both of them to their feet, the Eyes of Judgment becoming more vibrant.

"Cease your prattling. Now is your time of judgment."

They screamed.

* * * * * *

Antonio Vega sauntered into his expansive living room, a martini in each hand and a broad smile on his lips. He was a corpulent man, bald, aged in his late-fifties and was wearing a loose-fitting silk robe which barely covered his immense bulk. Before him, seated on the plush leather sofa, were a couple of bikini-clad babes, giggling at the mere sight of him.

"Here you are, my lovelies," he said with a wink. "Would you like anything more? Another line or three?" He snickered and gestured toward the massive glass coffee table, where the remains of a mass of white powder was visible.

Cocaine, obviously.

The Wraith pulled back from his vantage point outside on the balcony. He carefully retrieved a small listening device he had attached to the glass sliding door and placed it into his belt.

Vega was a small spider in Robert Latham's very large web of crime, but he was an important spider nonetheless. Vega was one of several men who distributed the drugs Latham imported onto the streets. He ensured the city's addicts were regularly fed and helped ensnare new prey to keep the profits growing. The Wraith had long tried to take Latham down, but the businessman had always proven too clever, too resourceful.

Latham covered his tracks and made sure he could not be connected to any part of his illicit activities. His legitimate business dealings were vast and useful to shroud his even vaster criminal empire. So, the Dread Avenger had resorted to taking down the smaller fish within Latham's organization. He hoped that by doing so he would both damage the criminal's drug and weapons trade and also enrage him, causing him to potentially make a mistake. When he did, The Wraith would be there, waiting.

The Wraith peered round the corner to take one last view of the proceedings. Vega was now seated in between the two ladies, an arm draped over each of them, a lascivious grin indicating what his intentions were. He wouldn't get the chance.

The Dread Avenger crashed through the balcony door, causing much panic and chaos inside. Shattered glass rained down on them and Vega himself shrieked like a stuck pig. He sprang to his feet in abject terror, leaving the two girls gripping each other for dear life on the sofa.

"Antonio Vega," The Wraith moaned. "Your time is at an end. It is your time of judgment." As he spoke, the Eyes of Judgment on his chest flared to life, crackling an intense, fiery yellow.

"No! Stay away from me!" Vega shrieked, backing up until he smacked into the wall at the far end of the room. Sweat trickled from his bald pate. "I'm a nothing, a small fry. It's Latham you want. Latham!"

"I want you both, Antonio," The Wraith said. "All who do evil in this city must ultimately face judgment. *My* judgment."

The sound of bare feet on the timber floor roused The Wraith from his anger and in a split-second, he whirled and let loose with a powerful backhand punch, which connected on the jaw of one of the ladies who had pathetically tried to sneak up on him, a vase in her hands. Her unconscious body slapped back onto the sofa. The vase shattered on the floor beside her.

"Do. Not. *Try!*" The Wraith warned the other girl, who hadn't moved from her spot on the sofa.

He turned back to face Vega, who was so afraid he too hadn't moved an inch. Vega trembled, drenched in sweat.

"Please, don't hurt me. It's Latham you want."

"You will be cleansed," The Wraith said, ignoring Vega. "You will feel the pain you have caused the poor souls of this city. And you will be the better for it."

He grabbed the hapless villain by the neck and pressed his face toward the Eyes of Judgment.

Vega screamed.

* * * * * *

Robert Latham parted the curtains at his study window and peered out into the night. The grounds of his vast estate were well lit and he could easily see much of his ornate Italianate garden. He smiled.

It must be over by now, he mused. *Poor Charlie. He had delusions of grandeur, to be sure, but he was a nice enough thug to kick around.*

There was a short knock and the door to his study opened slightly.

"Mr. Latham, sir?"

"Yes, come in."

A young man, younger and cleaner cut than Grieco, stepped inside. He was outfitted in an expensive Italian suit slightly too large for his slender frame. He looked eager to please.

"Yes, what is it, Jones?" Latham asked, having turned to face the young man.

"Our contact at the docks has reported in. Grieco and his crew have been arrested, his shipment impounded."

Latham smiled again. "Good, good. Everything went smoothly then."

"Yes," Jones said.

Latham rounded his wide, antique mahogany desk. "Jones, you've done well. You've shown some fine traits; obedience and loyalty. Keep it up and you'll go far within my organization. And always keep in mind the fate that befalls all that challenge me." His words bore some malice, despite the smile.

Jones nodded in eager compliance.

"You know, Jones," Latham continued, "I think you need to see my tailor. That suit just doesn't work for me. I'll call him in the morning, set up a meeting for you. If you're going to be my new right-hand man, you'll need to look the part at the very least. I'll arrange everything."

Jones looked a little surprised but said nothing, simply nodding once again.

"Good. You may go now. Get off home, get a good night's rest. Tomorrow is the start of something big for you."

"Thank you, sir," Jones said before exiting the study.

Latham stood before his mighty desk in silence, deep in thought. The Wraith had done him a favor this night. The irony of this amused him. He reached down to the beautifully enameled bronze cigar box on his desk and procured a specially rolled Cuban cigar from it. He removed the band, snipped the tip and lit it with a bejeweled lighter. He blew smoke rings from it as he walked slowly back to the bay window. Parting the curtains again, he once more looked out over his garden. He would repay The Wraith's good turn with one of his own.

He would kill him.

~ Also Available ~

The Wraith Adventures #1
THE WRAITH
Frank Dirscherl

In a world not far removed from our own, a city lies ravaged.
Crime overruns its streets; its citizens are helpless. Crime lord
Robert Latham, to the world at large a legitimate businessman,
holds the city in his sway. Fear and intimidation rule throughout.
One man stands above the rest, willing to fight for freedom.
That man is The Wraith.
ISBN: 978-0-646-90689-8

NOW AVAILABLE!

www.trinitycomics.com

The Wraith Adventures #2
VALLEY OF EVIL
Frank Dirscherl

After the horror the Cobra unleashed upon Metro City, Paul
Sanderson has recuperated, regained his strength and focus, and
the city has been rebuilt while its citizens have slowly started to
regroup and move forward. Into this relative calm marches Ma
Tzi, the Hong Kong drug lord, who senses a weakness in resident
crime lord Robert Latham's hold on the city and intends to
exploit that in any way necessary. And at any cost.
ISBN: 978-0-646-90809-0

NOW AVAILABLE!
www.trinitycomics.com

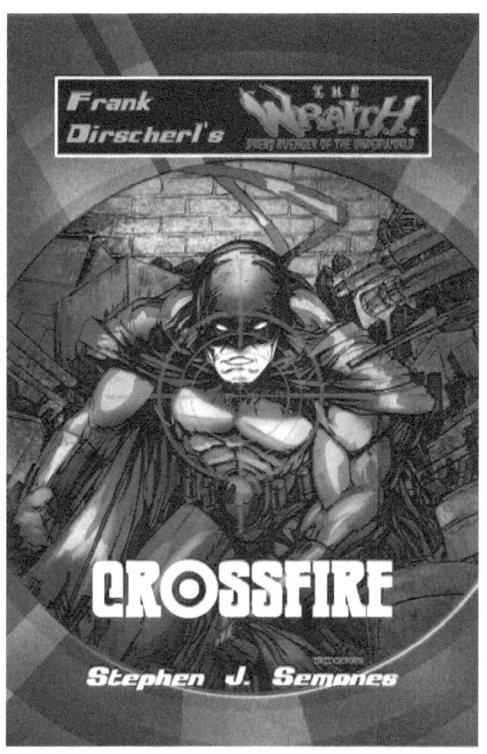

The Wraith Adventures #2.5
CROSSFIRE
Stephen J. Semones; edited by Frank Dirscherl

After a terrorist attack leaves the citizens of Metro City reeling, an
enigmatic stranger emerges from the wake of the destruction to
wage war on local crime-lord Robert Latham. In the midst of this,
Max Horton, The Wraith's right-hand man, vanishes without a
trace. Searching for Max, and for those responsible for the
devastation, The Wraith sets out for answers.

ISBN: 978-0-646-58377-8

NOW AVAILABLE!

www.trinitycomics.com

The Wraith Adventures #4
CRY OF THE WEREWOLF
Frank Dirscherl

Having gone through ordeal after ordeal, Paul Sanderson (aka The Wraith Dread Avenger of the Underworld ®) and his love Leena Patterson, decide to take a long overdue vacation. However, their idyll is soon shattered by an attack by a creature nobody thought could possibly exist—a werewolf. Soon, an evil so heinous makes himself known, and only The Wraith could possibly defeat it.
ISBN: 978-0-646-57757-9

AVAILABLE NOW!

www.trinitycomics.com

The Wraith comic book series

THE WRAITH: THE COLLECTED EDITIONS #1-3

Frank Dirscherl and a variety of artists

The adventures of the Dread Avenger of the Underworld in comic book format. The trade paperback collecting issues #1-3 of the series. Including each issue's color cover. Over 100 pages of action and excitement.
ISBN: 978-1-4710-4977-4

AVAILABLE NOW!

www.trinitycomics.com

Want to be The Wraith?

Well, it might be hard to actually *be* The Wraith, unless of course you, too, have been endowed with the power of the Eyes of Judgment. But you can certainly dress, drink and drive like him [*] (and you don't always have to be a millionaire to do so). See for yourselves.

The Wraith/Paul Sanderson wears:

- bespoke clothing from Shanghai
  C&G Fashion Ltd. –
  www.bespokesuit.en.ec21.com
- bespoke shoes from Shanghai
  Tianzi Shoes –
  www.aliexpress.com/fm-
  store/702551
- watches from Christopher Ward
  www.christopherward.co.uk

drinks:

- Twinings Earl & Lady Grey tea –
  www.twinings.co.uk
- The Balvenie Scotch whisky – www.thebalvenie.com
- Armand de Brignac champagne – www.armanddebrignac.com

uses:

- Toshiba laptops - www.toshiba.com
- Chesterfield furniture from Abbey Furniture
  www.chesterfieldfurnituremelbourne.com.au

drives:

- a Bentley Continental GT - www.bentleymotors.com

And, if you're really eager to actually look like The Wraith—in full costume—then you can always head over to Xtreme Design FX and let Lance Coulter there make you an exact replica of the costume used for The Wraith motion picture - www.xtremedesignfx.com

www.ingramcontent.com/pod-product-compliance
Lightning Source LLC
Chambersburg PA
CBHW050427260626
47156CB00003B/1190